"DO YOU STILL LIKE JELLY BEANS?" GABE asked softly.

Jessie smiled. "Sure. Do you still like tacos?"

He loved her voice, low and a bit gravelly. "Yep, the hotter the better."

She burst out laughing and fell back onto the blanket. Gabe couldn't stand it, and kissed her. She hadn't expected it. He hadn't meant to do it. Suddenly there was nothing but the beat of her heart and the roar of blood pulsing through her veins. For Jessie, every touch was magnified. Gabe's hair felt like silk between her fingers, and his lips smudged her skin with heated imprints. Her hands played across his chest, outlining the strong plains and valleys. "What's this?"

Her finger traced a fresh scar just south of his shoulder.

"It's nothing," he said casually, wincing as she pressed harder.

"Looks like a bullet wound to me," she said, touching her lips to the tender spot. "What kind of work do you do for the governor?"

"This and that," he muttered.

"I think you're the outlaw, Gabriel St. Clair, not me. You know, I always have a spot in my gang for a good man."

"What makes you think I'm good?" he asked, playfully pulling her close.

"I'm Jessie James." She laughed. "And I always recognize my own kind. Want to ride with me . . . ?"

WHAT ARE *LOVESWEPT* ROMANCES?

They are stories of true romance and touching emotion. We believe those two very important ingredients are constants in our highly sensual and very believable stories in the LOVESWEPT line. Our goal is to give you, the reader, stories of consistently high quality that may sometimes make you laugh, sometimes make you cry, but are always fresh and creative and contain many delightful surprises within their pages.

Most romance fans read an enormous number of books. Those they truly love, they keep. Others may be traded with friends and soon forgotten. We hope that each LOVESWEPT romance will be a treasure—a "keeper." We will always try to publish

LOVE STORIES YOU'LL NEVER FORGET
BY AUTHORS YOU'LL ALWAYS REMEMBER

The Editors

Loveswept ® 672

GABRIEL'S OUTLAW

SANDRA CHASTAIN

BANTAM BOOKS

NEW YORK · TORONTO · LONDON · SYDNEY · AUCKLAND

GABRIEL'S OUTLAW
A Bantam Book / March 1994

*LOVESWEPT and the wave design are registered
trademarks of Bantam Books, a division of
Bantam Doubleday Dell Publishing Group, Inc.
Registered in U.S. Patent
and Trademark Office and elsewhere.*

*If you would be interested in receiving protective vinyl covers for your
Loveswept books, please write to this address for information:*

Loveswept
Bantam Books
P.O. Box 985
Hicksville, NY 11802

ISBN 0-553-44442-5

Published simultaneously in the United States and Canada

Bantam Books are published by Bantam Books, a division of Bantam Doubleday Dell Publishing Group, Inc. Its trademark, consisting of the words
"Bantam Books" and the portrayal of a rooster, is Registered in U.S. Patent
and Trademark Office and in other countries. Marca Registrada. Bantam
Books, 1540 Broadway, New York, New York 10036.

PRINTED IN THE UNITED STATES OF AMERICA

OPM   0 9 8 7 6 5 4 3 2 1

For Lynn,
who always laughs
and makes the world
a happier place for those around her.

ONE

"Gabe, we've had a tip that a wagon train carrying gold is going to be held up. I'm assigning you to ride shotgun."

Gabriel St. Clair glared in disbelief at his baby-faced superior, the tough young head of the Georgia Bureau of Investigation. "This is the 1990s, Ben. Gold isn't moved by mules and wagons anymore."

"It is when the governor decides to reenact the wagon train that brought in the original forty-one ounces used to plate the dome on the state capitol."

"And somebody has threatened to hold up the gold train? You can't be serious," Gabe argued.

"I am serious. And you're the agent who is going to see that the gold is kept safe." Ben Jansen tried to smother a smile.

"Why me?" Gabe asked.

"You aren't ready to come back to full-time duty yet. So I'm giving you an easy assignment in your old hometown. A minivacation. Sorry you'll have to leave all those luscious nurses behind."

"A vacation?" Gabe didn't want to think about returning to Dahlonega. He would never consider it a vacation. He hadn't been back since he'd graduated from college, except for his father's funeral. He'd been out of the hospital for weeks, and there weren't any luscious nurses. He'd shied away from relationships ever since his broken engagement.

"Sure," his boss went on. "Think of it as horseback riding, camping out, getting away from the pressures of the city. You do ride, don't you?"

"Yes, but the original wagons were pulled by mules, not horses. Believe me, there's nothing easy about driving a team of mules seventy miles."

"You don't have to do the actual driving, Gabe, just tag along. The train already has a wagon master."

"And who is in charge?" Gabe asked, but he wasn't sure he wanted to know the answer.

Ben glanced down at the papers he was holding. "I'm told she's a dynamite-looking saloon owner named Jessie James. I believe her grandfather mined the gold originally."

That brought Gabriel to his feet. "Jessie James? You expect me to escort a gold train led by Jessie James? No way. I know Jessie personally."

Ben managed to keep a serious expression on his face as he explained. "A personal friend of the governor recommended you for the job because you *are* a friend of Miss James."

"Which personal friend would do that? I'll kill him."

"As a matter of fact it was Alice Magadan down at the Shelter for the Spiritual Odyssey of Man, you know that center for the homeless near the capitol. We were discussing the wagon train the other morning at breakfast when she reminded the governor that you were from Dahlonega."

"And since when do you and the governor discuss the assignments of your agents with an outsider?"

Ben looked amused. "Outsider? You know Alice Magadan, don't you?"

"Yes. I went to school with her son."

"Then you must know that between Alice and her sister, Jane, there's little that goes on over at the capitol that they don't know about."

Gabe groaned and sat back down. "Don't do this, Ben. You've heard of the Hatfields and the McCoys? Believe me, that feud was small potatoes compared to the one between the St. Clairs and the Jameses. It's been going on over two hundred years, ever since both claimed the same lot on Pumpkinvine Mountain in a land lottery, and they've never stopped."

Ben, still studying Gabe's file, let go a narrow smile that suggested he might know more than he was letting on about Gabe's relationship with Jessie.

"The sheriff of Lumpkin County has had a legitimate tip that the gold train is going to be held up, and because you're familiar with the people involved, he's approved our sending you along."

Gabe crossed his arms over his chest and winced at the tender spot where the bullet that had put him out of commission had entered his shoulder. "I won't do it!" he said in a low voice. "I'll take that vacation."

"Too late. I've already told the governor you'd go."

"I don't know why anybody is doing this. How much is the gold worth anyhow?"

"You'll be carrying fourteen ounces, worth about three hundred and fifty dollars an ounce."

"Why not send a state patrol car or an armored truck?" Gabe argued.

"We could send an armored car," Ben agreed, "but moving the gold down here is a symbolic gesture. The gold originally came here from the James mine by wagon train. As part of their Gold Rush Days Celebration, they're going to reenact the wagon trip."

Gabe could see that he wasn't going to change his supervisor's mind. The governor thought it was a good public-relations gesture, and Gabe happened to be recovering from a gunshot wound. His doctor wouldn't release him for hazardous duty yet, but Ben thought that driving a wagon train for seventy miles would be a piece of cake.

A piece of fruitcake, Gabe thought, trying to find a way out, trying and giving up in frustration. It wasn't the assignment that was bothering him. It was Jessie.

Jessie James. There had never been another daredevil like her. And it was all her grandfather Alston's fault. He'd filled her head with tales of the outlaw who made the name Jesse James famous, and she'd tried to live up to it.

Gabe could still remember their childhood friendship. She'd followed him as a skinny little girl, then later as a twelve-year-old who spit fire and threw elbows one minute in a pickup basketball game, and the next minute turned modest at the idea of swimming in their underwear.

Oh, she'd never been a real outlaw, not the kind who broke the law, but she'd gone her own way. While other girls had fallen in love with makeup and rock stars, Jessie had fished and hunted. Eventually, she'd even become her father's gambling buddy, until she'd been arrested for disturbing the peace when her father hadn't wanted to leave a poker game and the St. Clairs had refused to take his IOUs.

Ben snapped the file folder closed. "I understand that you haven't been back to Dahlonega since you signed on with the bureau. Is that right?"

"That's right. The St. Clair family hasn't always followed the letter of the law. I didn't want to take a chance on having to arrest one of my forty-second cousins for making moonshine or fighting chickens. Folks in that part of the country are still fiercely loyal to their own kin. They never let you forget."

"You have forty-two cousins?"

"Of course not. Forty-second cousin is a mountain expression to explain why everybody who's ever married a relative, no matter how distant, claims kin to you if it is to their advantage."

"That's a relief." Ben swallowed a smile. "I want you looking for robbers, not defending family."

"I have only one uncle and three male cousins left in Dahlonega now, and unless Uncle Buck has taken up robbing wagon trains, I think we're safe."

Ben frowned. "I was told it isn't common knowledge in Dahlonega that you're an officer in the Georgia Bureau of Investigation."

"No, they don't know I'm a GBI agent. After I got my degree, I signed on with you guys. Once

I graduated from the academy, I avoided Lumpkin County. Is that a problem?"

"Not at all. In fact, we think it would be better if you just tell Miss James that you've been sent by the secretary of state to join the train as a liaison officer."

"Being dishonest with Jessie could be a mistake, Ben."

"Maybe, but if the thieves don't know you're in law enforcement, they might give themselves away."

"Won't it seem a little odd when an outsider turns up?"

"Not at all. The local newspaper has already reported that the governor is sending a representative to oversee the ride."

Gabe groaned. "You mean, not only do I have to play Clint Eastwood, I have to oversee a bunch of real tenderfeet driving real Conestoga wagons down real highways in real traffic? Some vacation."

"One Conestoga wagon," Ben corrected. "A gift from the state of Pennsylvania for the Centennial celebration. Don't worry, Gabe. I'm sure you'll do fine. And Gabe," he added as his officer started to leave, "don't forget, you're there to protect the gold. That isn't a joke."

No, Gabe thought, the joke was on him.

Gabriel St. Clair had to play guardian angel to the most headstrong outlaw he'd ever known, Jessie James.

Jessie could see only a silhouette of the Stetson-clad man as he walked across the dark saloon, threading his way between the tables. He leaned on the bar, adjacent to the life-size cardboard figure of a blond country singer selling a popular beer, and waited.

A long, tense minute passed. "Anyone here?" he called out.

The timbre of his voice had deepened; it was warm and smooth, like polished mahogany. Her pulse responded instantly like wind chimes dancing just beneath her skin. Her chest tightened. Her mouth went dry.

Jessie had seen all kinds in the Gold Dust Saloon, but there'd never been anyone else so confident in boots and blue jeans. He could have been a space ranger off one of those new television programs, or a country singer looking for work. But this man, whatever he'd become, was secure about himself in a way he never had been before.

"Hello?" he called out, his voice rising in question.

Jessie, standing behind in the darkened door-way at the other end of the bar, gave a silent oath and looked around for Nathan, the old-timer who tended bar. But, as usual, whenever she needed him, he was nowhere to be found. She couldn't run; the past had caught up with her.

She squared her shoulders and took a deep breath. As owner of the struggling country-music dance hall and saloon, she knew that keeping customers happy was essential, no matter who they were, even if they did turn up before opening time. Jessie swallowed the lump threatening to close off her windpipe and sallied forth. She could handle this, she told herself, she was an adult now. She was Jessie James.

Gabriel St. Clair drummed his fingertips on the bar and wondered what he'd done to be punished in this way. Taking an undercover assignment was fine, but to be sent back to his own hometown, to face his uncle, to face Jessie, was asking too much. But suddenly there she was, heading for him like a Mack truck out of control, and he braced himself for the collision.

"I'm sorry, sir, but we're not open yet. I'll have to ask you to come back later."

She was wearing an oversized man's shirt, a pair of army fatigues, and running shoes that no self-respecting jogger would be caught dead in. No other woman would wear such an outfit and stand beside the cutout of Tanya Tucker, who some considered the foxiest lady in country music.

Not unless she had raven-black hair that gleamed like velvet. Not unless her skin was the shade of Old World porcelain, and she had hot-chocolate eyes. Not unless she carried a hunting knife on her belt and had a .357 Magnum in plain sight on the counter. Not unless she was the infamous Jessie James.

Gabe watched as Jessie's foot hit a slick spot, and she slammed into the cardboard figure. He moved quickly around the bar to come to her assistance. Suddenly, he and Jessie James were doing the Texas Two-Step with Tanya Tucker wedged between them.

"Damn!" Jessie swore. The display hadn't been free. She'd bought it to draw the men into the dance hall. Now Tanya was about to develop some wrinkles that didn't come with age.

"Jessie, did you call me?" The absent Nathan suddenly appeared, took one look at his employer, and blinked in disbelief. "Unhand that woman, son."

"Sorry," Gabe said, making certain that Jessie had her footing and stepping back. "I wasn't trying to take advantage of Miss James."

"Never thought you were," Nathan observed, taking the display of the leather-clad woman in hand and shaking his head sadly. "Jessie would eat you for breakfast if she wanted to. It's Tanya who's in danger."

Nathan repositioned the cardboard cutout, gave it a couple of intimate caresses, and left the room.

"Hello, Gabe. The bar isn't open yet," Jessie said, wiping her shoe with a sheet from a roll of paper towels.

"I don't want a drink. I'm here officially," Gabe answered.

She hadn't changed, he thought. She still jutted out her chin and challenged all comers. But there was more: An energy shimmered between them that he didn't remember before. Jessie had become a James, ready to take on Gabe as a St. Clair, and he wasn't prepared for that. He'd have to tread carefully.

Officially? Jessie might have been calmer if she hadn't been reeling from the effect of his touch. "Officially? What in hell are you talking about?"

"You don't want to hear this, but I'm the governor's representative on the wagon train. I know this won't be easy, Jessie, but I'll be gone in a week, and you can pretend you never laid eyes on me. Do you think we can forget about what happened in the past?"

Memories set her senses reeling, memories of the lake, smoky bonfires, deep, sensual kisses, and the pain of one fall afternoon when Gabriel St. Clair had destroyed her dreams forever.

Regret sliced into her. She'd thought that she had forgotten. She didn't want to remember. She wouldn't. Bravely, she raised her lashes and let her gaze ride up his body to his face.

Gabe pushed his hat back to reveal the same strong face she'd memorized in junior high.

She was still holding the paper towel she'd used to wipe her shoe. Now, she jammed it somewhere in the vicinity of her pocket, missed, and watched it flutter to the floor. "Damn you, Gabe St. Clair!" she swore, then wished she could call it back.

She'd done it again, given herself away. She was still a thirteen-year-old, and he was still the quarterback on the football team embarrassed by the awkward, moonstruck kid with a crush as big as the mountain on which they'd both lived.

Jessie jerked the rubber band from around her ponytail, recaptured the escaping strands, and let it snap back into place.

"Just think of me as your guardian angel, Jessie, here to protect you and your gold," Gabe said with a grim smile.

Jessie's lips were full and naturally red. They were practically trembling now with fury. "Your name may be Gabriel, but you're no angel. You were a thief ten years ago, and I'm willing to bet you still are. So, why are you really here?"

He couldn't argue with her. She was right. Like his infamous grandfather, he had stolen from Jessie

James. He'd stolen the most precious thing she'd had to give, her innocence and her trust. And she hadn't forgotten. Neither had he. "Ten years ago I was only a twenty-two-year-old kid."

"And I was only eighteen. So, you're an old man now. Well, you can tell Lonnie and Jane that I don't need any help."

"I know. You can handle the job all by yourself. Sorry, but I don't know any Lonnie and Jane. This assignment came straight from the governor. I was told to get Jessie and the gold to town!"

"Of course, the angel Gabriel only takes his orders from the highest authority."

"This is no joke, Jessie. Believe me, if I'd been able to get out of the assignment, I would have. I deserve anything you want to say. I don't blame you for being bitter."

"Try furious. Try teed-off big time. Try turning around and taking your tight little buns back to wherever you've been resting them for the last ten years."

"Tight buns?" This was the Jessie he remembered.

Jessie watched as the boyish grin curled his lips, the one he'd let loose when there was no one else around. His weight was less bulky now, allowing his clothes to hug his lithe body in that special way of an athlete. Maybe his hair was a bit darker, though it was still streaked light by the sun as it had been every summer when they'd swum in the lake. But it was the eyes that stopped her examination, wicked blue eyes that had always seen straight through her and made her resort to extremes in an attempt to prove that she was indifferent to his charm. She couldn't stay angry with him, even when she tried.

"Okay, Wyatt Earp," she snapped, "you have gun, will travel. You're offering. But I'm not buying."

He planted one snakeskin boot on the bar rail as the smile vanished. "Jessie, I'm being paid by the state to ride along. Just to make sure you don't lose the gold along the way."

That stopped her. He didn't have to remind her that the Jameses were famous for losing their gold.

"This James gold has been stored in the vault of the Bank of Dahlonega for over forty years," Jessie said in that familiar low, gravelly voice that he remembered so well. "I don't intend to lose it now, and I don't intend to let a St. Clair get his hands on it either."

"Jessie, darling, is he here yet?" Jane Short, a pint-sized octogenarian wearing a short gingham square-dance costume and white Shirley Temple shoes with taps, scurried into the bar. "Lonnie saw a tall, handsome cowboy asking the sheriff's deputy about you. If he's the governor's man, he may be just what the doctor ordered."

"Jane, he may be what the doctor ordered, but if I ordered a man, it would be a cold day in hell before it would be a St. Clair."

Jane looked confused. "Oh, dear. And Alice thought he was so perfect. Lonnie told me not to get my hopes up, but I was sure the tarot cards said that an outlaw would meet an angel. Good and evil. Yin and yang. What do you mean a St. Clair?" Jane came toward the bar, caught sight of Gabe, and stopped. "Hello. I knew it. If Jessie's the outlaw, you must be the angel. What's your name?"

"Gabriel St. Clair, ma'am."

"Jessie and Gabriel. Perfect."

There'd been a time when Jessie had thought the same thing, when she'd scrawled JESS AND GABE inside a heart, block-printed it in neat letters on a book cover, and scripted it with a quill in black India ink around the edges of her composition books in junior high. That was before Gabe's buddies started to tease him about her crush, before Gabe fell in love with Laura Redding.

At that moment Nathan turned on the light switch. The old western saloon atmosphere was lost in the play of strobe lights and pulsating golden neon. The jukebox was blaring a Garth

Brooks song suggesting he had friends in low places.

Gabriel shook his head in disbelief. "Angel? To tell you the truth, ma'am, I'm not at all sure. Maybe you can give me a clue. When you travel with Jessie James, you never know whether you're in heaven or hell."

TWO

The Saturday crowd of tourists flocked along the wide brick sidewalks, moving in and out of the restored shops that made up the square around the old courthouse, now a gold museum. A lot had happened in the years Gabe had been away. He didn't remember the downtown area looking so prosperous and alive.

And he didn't remember ever walking that far in Dahlonega without someone recognizing him. Now, he was glad to be anonymous. He badly need to think. Seeing Jessie again had knocked the props out from under his neat, controlled life. They weren't old friends anymore, but he hadn't thought they were enemies either. He wasn't sure what they were, and he didn't like not being in control.

Pondering the changes he was encountering,

Gabe St. Clair made his way past the old feed-and-seed store toward the sheriff's office. He'd been out earlier.

For as long as he could remember, the St. Clairs and the Jameses lived for the moment, trusting God or good fortune to see them through instead of being responsible for their own lives. Nobody in town had much use for the two families, until he'd become the quarterback of the football team. Suddenly, even the beautiful Laura Redding had become interested in him. He hadn't been just that wild kid from the mountain any longer. He'd been accepted into the inner circle of the popular kids. And he hadn't wanted Jessie tagging after him. He still felt shame at the way he'd treated Jessie in front of his new friends.

But she'd never held that against him, never let her hurt show. Instead, she'd begun to keep her distance in public, waiting for him to seek her out. Until that last summer, before he left for college, when Laura had dropped him for a law student whose father was the mayor. When school was over and Gabe wasn't on the team anymore, his friends had no longer sought him out. He'd known then that he'd always be that kid from Pumpkinvine Mountain. There was no place in which he belonged.

Except with Jessie. He could still remember those summer days. Jessie sitting on the dock, her huge dark eyes wide with concern as she trailed her bare feet in the water, listening to his tale of heartbreak. At night they'd build a campfire to keep the mosquitoes away, and the smoke would drift over the water.

Jessie had listened to him, trying hard to understand his explanation of his fears and his thwarted desire, of his shame over his family and their lack of ambition and his determination to get far away from Pumpkinvine Mountain. She'd listened and said she'd understood his desire to leave, though she could never be happy anywhere else.

Then one night, giving in to the need to be comforted, he'd laid his head in Jessie's lap, closed his eyes, and pretended she was Laura.

When Jessie had kissed him, he'd responded, responded and deepened the kiss as he'd done so often with Laura. Night after night, Laura had pushed him away, but Jessie hadn't.

He'd discovered that the body he touched was no longer boyish and lean. The breasts he'd held were lush, the nipples hard, and the pulse in the hollow of her neck had raced beneath his touch.

Jessie James had grown up, and he hadn't noticed. And she was letting him know that he was still the star in her heavens and the object of her desire.

He'd been stunned at what he'd done and what he'd wanted to do. Jessie was his friend, not his girl. "Damn! What are you doing, Jessie? You're a child—not a—not some—pull down your shirt!"

Horrified, Gabe pulled away, leaving Jessie confused and hurt by his rejection.

The next day he'd left for college, surprised to find that it was Jessie he had to put out of his mind, not Laura. After that he only returned to the mountain for a family emergency. From time to time he caught sight of Jessie, but he didn't seek her out. Jessie meant the mountain, and the mountain meant pain. It was only now that he was beginning to understand that he'd blamed Jessie for something she couldn't have changed.

He knew that he'd used her as a substitute for the girl he'd wanted, and worse, he'd hidden his friendship with her. A teenaged boy who shared his innermost thoughts with a little girl would have been made fun of by his friends. And they would have taunted Jessie unmercifully.

Taunted, or made use of her innocence. As he later had.

The sheriff was sitting behind his desk, his swivel chair turned away from the door, when Gabe knocked.

"Come in," he said, turning around and coming to his feet. "Hello, Gabe, good to see you. Sorry I missed you earlier."

"Joey? Joey St. Clair? You can't be the sheriff!"

"Why? Is there some reason that there can't be two St. Clairs in law enforcement?"

"Why, no. Of course not. I'm just surprised, that's all." Gabe shook hands with his oldest cousin and accepted his invitation to sit down.

"You mean that you're surprised that a member of a family that produced more moonshiners and gamblers than law-abiding citizens could give up his shady past and reform."

"No, I mean yes. I guess I am." He was surprised. Of the three cousins Joey had been the one least likely to turn over a new leaf, and he wouldn't have given a fig for any one of them. "I didn't know you'd been elected sheriff."

"And I didn't know about you being with the bureau, until your boss called. We had a good laugh when he asked me to keep it quiet. Have you seen Uncle Buck?"

"Nope. I just got into town."

"You ought to go, Gabe. He misses you."

"You mean he misses my money."

Joey gave him an odd look. "Probably, he always did know how to take advantage of an opportunity. But I think he'd be pleased if you'd stop by. He's getting old and more crotchety than ever, now that the family's coming down off the mountain. You know him; he doesn't like change, and he likes outsiders even less."

"He's like kudzu. Before you know it, he

can strangle you." It had been Uncle Buck—and his conviction that families stayed together and shared their troubles and their fortunes—who had sent Gabe away. "What about Cousin Walter and Cousin Ralph?"

"Ralph has a job with the new brewery down in Cartersville, and Walter's still farming the James place. Though I've heard talk about his selling it."

"Married?"

"Yes, me included. What about you, Gabe?"

"No, I'm not married. I've been working too hard for that. About the gold," he said, changing the subject as he tried to assimilate the news that the St. Clairs had changed their colors, "is there really a threat to the gold?"

"There's a threat all right, Gabe. I took the call myself. He said that somebody intended to steal the gold, and he was just warning us so the town wouldn't look bad."

"He?" Gabe asked.

The sheriff looked surprised. "Well, now, I assumed it was a he, but the voice was disguised. Could have been a woman, I guess. But the only woman around here with balls enough to do something like that is—"

"Jessie James," Gabe finished his sentence, then stared at Joey in disbelief. "You don't think that Jessie would stage a holdup, do you?"

"No, I don't, not and spoil her family name. But everybody knows she needs money pretty bad."

"Why does Jessie need money? Isn't her saloon doing a good business?"

"Yeah, but she mortgaged that last strip of land to make the down payment on her saloon, and it took every penny she had to remodel. Now, she's behind on her loan. Seems like our stock went up as hers went down."

"Who does Jessie think made the call?"

The sheriff laughed, pulling out a cigar and biting off the end of it. "She thinks it was one of the St. Clairs. You know how our families have always been. If something happens to one, we blame it on the other."

Gabe let out an exasperated oath. "Why would one of the St. Clairs want to rob the wagon train?"

"We wouldn't. Oh, I wouldn't put it past Uncle Buck to threaten to do it, but he wouldn't call. He'd know that I'd recognize his voice."

As much as he hated the idea, Gabe decided that, in the line of duty, he'd have to call on his uncle before he worked out a plan. When he was satisfied that he had learned everything Joey knew, he started back down the street.

"Gabe! Gabe!" The woman from the bar came tapping down the street behind him. "Hold up!"

He turned and waited, curious about this outsider who talked about yin and yang.

"I'm sorry if I sounded like an idiot back there. Just because I know a thing to be true doesn't mean that others will understand. I hope you're not offended."

"No, ma'am. I'm not offended. But pairing Jessie and me off is going to take more than yin and yang."

"Nonsense! It's obvious that she's crazy about you. By the way, I'm Jane Couples Short. I think you know my nephew, Gavin."

"Yes, ma'am."

"I told Lonnie, when I asked him to marry me, that it would be better if he took my name. Couples just sounds more permanent than Short, but he refused. It's a man thing, I suppose. Are you intimidated by that kind of thing?"

Gabe shook his head. Though he wasn't entirely sure he understood a word she'd said.

"Oh, I'm confusing you. I'm good at that. But"—she smiled impishly—"that's what keeps the sex interesting, don't you think? I mean, you'd be surprised what tap dancing does for the libido."

She demonstrated a few steps, then gave a curtsy and winked. "Have dinner with us tonight at the saloon. Jessie's going to sing her new song."

That caught Gabe's attention. He'd never known Jessie could sing. "I don't think Jessie would like that."

"Ah, that's where you're wrong. Have you ever seen the New Guinea fighting flapdoodle hen?"

"Can't say that I have."

"What they do is flap their wings and let out a screech that will curl your hair. Then they physically attack the rooster of their choice. If he puts up a good-enough fight, they mate for life. I think Jessie is like that."

"If that's what leads up to the mating process, I doubt that rooster's life is very long."

Jane grinned. "Maybe not, but they die a glorious death. Come to dinner, Gabe."

"If I turn up uninvited at your dinner table, I might never have the chance to find out about that glorious kind of life."

"You never know until you try."

Moments later, without quite knowing how it had happened, Gabe had accepted Jane Short's invitation to dinner and her recommendation that he get a room in the Nugget Hotel across the street.

He headed for his Jeep to claim his duffel bag. Even though he thought he'd been prepared, seeing Jessie again had caught him off guard. Time hadn't erased the bond between them. If anything, it had grown. Or maybe it had only taken the memories of their shared past to revive it.

Now, he'd have to force himself to forget about his time with Jessie, about bare legs in lake-green water and smoky kisses. That had been a time of anger and confusion for them, of hormones and emotions. Since then they'd both grown up. When he was eighteen, he'd done the right thing and refused what Jessie had wanted to give. Four years later Jessie had been the one to send him away.

Jessie listened idly while the musicians tuned their instruments and set up the stage. Her thoughts were scattered. Memories of Gabe overwhelmed her, forcing her to think about what might have been at a time when she ought to— no, absolutely needed to—deal with the present.

The autumn tourist season was in full swing. Carloads of families drove north to see the Blue Ridge Mountains turning red and gold.

There would be a good crowd tonight. Lord knew, she needed a good crowd. She was the only one who knew how empty her bank account was. She'd used most of the summer-season money to pay ahead on the operational costs of her saloon. Once winter came, the bar would eke out a meager existence from the few locals who remained and an odd hunter or two, but the big spenders wearing new boots and western shirts wouldn't come.

Boots and blue jeans. Stetson hats. Gabriel St. Clair.

Jessie's breathing tightened as she replayed the events of the morning in her head. She'd lost Gabe long ago, but she'd thought she'd gotten over him; she was wrong about that. Still, even a James learned to get on with living. Instead of drawing hearts around Gabe's name, she'd made him the focus of her fury, the yardstick by which she measured her success.

Gabe was the first St. Clair to graduate from college. After that, he'd distanced himself from his family and the mountain, just as he'd so desperately wanted.

Jessie was the first James to get a degree, returning to the mountain to reclaim what her family had lost. And she'd been a failure—until now. The Gold Dust Saloon was finally beginning to show a profit. It was the mountain land and her dream of buying back the farm that she was in danger of losing.

"Hey, Jessie, listen to this." Mike, one of the musicians, played a melancholy refrain on the piano. "It's the ending of our new song."

"Sounds good," she said, drawing her attention away from Gabriel and the past. The saloon was filling with customers who wanted to dance and drink. She needed to inventory the stock and replenish the necessary items.

"I thought we'd do the song tonight."

"No!" Jessie hadn't meant to shout; the refusal

had leaped from her mouth before she'd realized it was happening. "Later, maybe."

"Later won't do," Mike said quietly. "The man from that new Nashville record company is coming to hear us."

"Oh, Mike. I'm sorry. Are you sure?"

"That's what I was told. It was going to be a surprise. But, hey, we can always do something else. We're great, even without your song."

Jessie walked over to the tiny stage and leaned against the back of the old upright piano. "No, the song is good, maybe the best thing we've written. We'll do it. Let's hear the ending."

Moments later she was singing, her deep, throaty voice pouring through the open doors, belting out the pain of lost love, halting the steps of the tourists passing the bar.

The sound of her voice brought Gabriel St. Clair, who was halfway into the hotel, to a sudden stop.

"She's great, isn't she? Nobody can sing about hurting like Jessie," the man sweeping off the sidewalk said.

"That's Jessie?"

"Yep. You must be Gabe. I'm Lonnie, Jane's husband."

"Jane, the woman who thought you ought to become a couple instead of being short?"

Lonnie looked at Gabe curiously, then let out

a laugh. "I can't believe you understood what she was saying. Most people just scratch their head and keep going."

"I didn't understand, until now. And I like her, though she's way out in left field about Jessie and me."

"You'll find that Jane has a way of moving the field if it isn't where she wants it to be. Look at me. Here I am, a retired diesel mechanic, running a tourist hotel and taking up square dancing."

He'd heard about Aunt Jane from her nephew Gavin. He still wasn't sure what she was doing in Dahlonega, but her reputation for being unpredictable made anything believable, including the New Guinea flapdoodle hen.

Jessie's voice had dropped. Gabriel could no longer understand the words, only the suggestion of her pain, pain they'd once shared. And then he was remembering Jessie in his arms that morning, with only a sheet of cardboard between them. Jessie, all grown up. Jessie, the woman.

What was different about Jessie now? Hell, he hadn't lusted after Jessie back then; she'd just been a substitute for Laura. He couldn't reconcile a childhood friendship with the stirrings of desire that he'd felt earlier that morning, with the ache in his heart when he'd heard her voice.

Gabe shifted the bag he'd flung over his shoulder and realized that Lonnie was staring at him expectantly. He must have missed something. "Tell me this, Lonnie," he said quickly, trying to cover his confusion, "is there such a thing as a New Guinea flapdoodle hen?"

"Couldn't say, but if Jane told you she's cooking one for dinner, you might want to have a snack before you come."

The dance floor of the Gold Dust Saloon, a large square area two steps lower than the tables that overlooked it, was packed with western-garbed dancers going through an intricate series of steps in perfect time to the music.

"When I was a kid, this place was a disco," Gabe said to Lonnie, who was watching Jane dancing with a stranger.

"Bet you and Jessie made quite a couple."

"Jessie and I never danced."

Then he remembered. They had danced, once. He'd tried to teach her how, got his feet tangled, and crashed both of them to the dock where they'd been practicing. They'd laughed and decided that athletes and musicians used up all their rhythm and didn't have any left for dancing.

They'd laughed. He and Jessie had always laughed. Gabe shook his head. He ought to be on the phone with the bureau, coordinating their efforts, running a check on known thieves in the area. Instead, he was listening to the music wind down as the lights dimmed to spotlight a stool onstage.

Then Jessie stepped into the glow, and Gabe swallowed the last of his drink with a loud gulp. She was wearing the dress of a dance-hall girl from the 1800s, pink, with black lace trim and a slit up the side that allowed her to cross one shapely fishnet-clad leg seductively over the other. She was a sensual woman, and his pulse thudded.

"Good evening, ladies and gentlemen. Welcome to the Gold Dust Saloon. These long-legged guitar players behind me are called the Dusters, and I'm Jessie James. Tonight we'd like to sing a song I wrote about a girl who hid her love for the man who used her and walked away."

Gabriel didn't think that Jessie knew he was there, but she appeared to be looking directly at him as she began to sing. It was the same song he'd heard that afternoon. Except now he could understand the words.

> *"There's another woman inside of me.*
> *I've kept her hidden so no one can see.*
> *But she's driving me crazy.*
> *Crazy.*
> *. . . I thought that he was locked away.*

Away to stay in yesterday.
Until I saw him.
Now I'm that woman inside of me.
Yesterday's love has broken free.
And I'm going crazy.
Crazy."

There wasn't a sound in the house. She had every one of them in the palm of her hand, and they shared every feeling she had. Even Gabe felt the pain.

He wanted to walk across that floor and comfort her as she'd done for him so long ago, to tell her that everything would be okay. To hold her again.

Then the lights came on, and the crowd went wild.

Jessie gave a quick bow, blew the audience a kiss, and disappeared into the crowd, appearing moments later behind Lonnie.

"Jane, what do you think of the finished product?"

Then she caught sight of Gabriel, and her face lost the little color it had. For a moment she swayed, then visibly caught herself and nodded. "Hello, Gabe. I didn't know you were a fan of country music."

"I didn't know it either. But I liked that song

very much. I didn't know you were a singer," Gabe said, raising his voice to be heard over the music.

"I'm not. I just fool around with the band. I'm the cheapest singer I know. And cheap is important around here."

"You know, Lonnie," Jane suddenly said, "I've got a sudden urge for Chinese food. I hope you won't mind if we leave you two alone, will you, Gabe?"

"Oh, no, you don't," Jessie said, blocking Jane's exit. "You came for dinner, and you're going to stay and eat."

"I don't think I'm in the mood for guinea hens," Jane said. "But Gabe here looks like a man who is starving to death. And you've definitely got your feathers flapping."

Before either Jessie or Gabe knew what had happened, they were alone at the table. Before either could comment, two dancers had dropped into the vacant chairs and turned them toward the band.

"So much for privacy," Gabe observed.

"Guinea hen? I don't know what all that business was about, but the only thing we serve in here is steak and burgers. And there's nothing private about it."

Jessie had never worn lipstick before. Now her burgundy-colored lips were parted in a full pout.

The woman standing before him was no longer a long-legged, skinny kid. She was a fantasy, an erotic fantasy that cinched his stomach muscles and stole his breath.

"I don't think I'm very hungry anyway, Jessie. What I'd rather do is find somewhere quiet where we can talk."

"I don't think we have anything to talk about, Gabe." She was still rocked by walking into Gabe just as she'd finished singing about a woman seeing the man she'd once loved. Maybe it was because she was still caught up in the song that she was having trouble hiding her emotions.

Gabe saw the misery in her eyes and wished he didn't feel responsible for putting it there. There had been a time when they hadn't tried to conceal their feelings, when they could tell each other everything. At least he'd told her his feelings, and she'd always listened.

"I think maybe we do, Jessie." We have ten years to get through, he wanted to say; instead he heard himself lamely falling back on official duties. "We need to talk about outlaws and gold heists."

"Not tonight," she said, backing away into the dancers and losing herself in the crowd. Jessie worked her way around toward the bar, ducked into a doorway beside it, and hurried up the steps.

Nathan and the other bartenders could handle things for a while. She needed air, and space, and time to gather her thoughts.

She needed the woman she'd sung about to crawl back inside her protective shell. She needed to stop the crazy patter of her heart.

She wasn't about to get any of it. No sooner had she reached the roof of the saloon than she heard footsteps behind her.

It was Gabe. She knew before she turned. He walked toward her, stopped, and for a moment she thought that he was going to kiss her, wished for it, as fire ignited in her stomach and exploded through her body.

She turned away, swallowing the lump in her throat that threatened to close off her breathing. "Go away, Gabe. I don't want you here."

"Why not? I thought we were old friends?"

"No, we're not friends, not anymore. And this, whatever this is between us, is new."

"And you won't let anything new into your life, will you, Jessie? You're still hanging on to the past as if you're afraid you'll disappear if you don't."

"Go away," she said in a tight voice. "I am the past—your past—and you don't want any part of it. You've made that very clear."

"I'm sorry I stayed away, Jessie, without explaining why."

"You don't owe me any explanations, Gabe. I don't want anything from you."

He didn't believe her. The want had been there in her dark eyes earlier that morning in the bar, and moments ago, before she'd turned away to hide those betraying eyes. "I don't believe you, Jessie. We can't hide our feelings from each other. We never could. I want to kiss you, and I think you want me too." Slowly, he turned her around and pulled her into his arms.

She was right, this feeling was different. She closed her eyes and parted her lips. He lowered his head, gently touching his lips to hers.

And the past fell away.

THREE

There hadn't been a time in the last ten years when Jessie hadn't envisioned this meeting, this outcome, this kiss. Envisioned and angrily erased.

She'd finally relegated Gabriel St. Clair to the past. He'd made it abundantly clear that she didn't mean anything to him ten years before and nothing had happened since to change her mind.

Until he kissed her.

Then every thought of being sensible flew right out of her head. She was pressing herself against him, reveling in the strong, hard feel of him, in the weakness of her knees and the hot tickle of his tongue inside her mouth.

His hand slid across her shoulder and down the small of her back, pulling her closer. "I know this is a mistake," he said, feathering hungry kisses across her upper lip. "But I don't seem to be able to stop myself."

"I don't play games anymore, Gabe."

"Neither do I."

"I don't believe you," she said, looking up into blue eyes that were flint-hard in the shadowy night. "What do you want from me?"

He gave a half-laugh, wondering that himself. "Want? Emotionally, I don't think I can answer that. Physically? I believe it's pretty obvious."

She pulled away. "You'd still rather be anywhere else than here, hadn't you? But you kiss me, and your body seems to have a different preference."

"Yes, it does," he answered reluctantly. "You seem to have that effect on me."

"So, we make love, and then what? You disappear for another ten years? What are you, some kind of locust who returns to feed in cycles? If that's what you're doing, don't, Gabe. I'm not available anymore."

"I deserve that," he admitted, feeling like the bad boy he'd always been accused of being.

But he didn't deserve the blame. Jessie knew she'd been available the last time they'd met. She couldn't turn him away then, but she had to do it now. She had to make him think that her feelings were dead and buried, for she couldn't survive being left again. Taking slow, deep breaths, she allowed exposed nerve endings to draw into a coil of desperate anger, and then, quite deliberately, she reached out and slapped him.

Gabriel, momentarily surprised, released her slowly. He narrowed his lips and took a step back. "I'm sorry. I owe you an apology. But I thought that you were as involved in whatever just happened as I."

"I was just surprised!" she snapped. But he was right. The moment he'd touched her she'd melted, melted and invited him to take whatever he wanted.

"No more than I," he managed. "I'm sorry. We seem to have gotten off to a bad start. I certainly didn't have this in mind when I followed you." He rubbed his face, then turned and walked over to the waist-high brick facade that ran around the roof of the saloon.

He expelled a deep breath. "Listen, Jessie, this new—whatever it is—has come as a big surprise to me too. I convinced myself that what happened ten years ago was just part of growing up, of hormones, of being different from the rest of the people we ran with. I didn't mean to hurt you, and I didn't know what to do when I had."

"I know, Gabe. You're right. I'm sorry too. It was just—just—that you were my first love. Everybody remembers that one, makes more of it than it was."

"I suppose." But dammit, he hadn't wanted to think of Jessie that way. He couldn't. It gave emotion a hold on his determination to leave. She was a part of the mountain and the pain of his childhood. They'd always wanted different things. He'd wanted to go, and she'd wanted to stay. Still he remembered her song, and he couldn't stop himself from asking. "Was I the man who walked away?"

"Certainly not. Only an egotistical jerk would think such a thing. You aren't the only man in my life. Besides, I sent you away."

"I'm probably the only jerk dumb enough to allow myself to walk away from Jessica James twice. Maybe I wasn't as smart as I thought I was."

"Maybe you weren't," she said softly.

She done it, she'd pushed him away by slapping his face, made him believe that her response had come from latent nostalgia, the reliving of a childish daydream, pent-up emotion.

Gabe leaned his arms over the white filigreed trim on top of the rail and stared across the town toward the mountains. He was confused by what had happened. To give himself time to recover, he fell back on his assignment. "Why would someone want to steal your gold?"

"I don't know. Why don't you tell me."

"Joey says you think the St. Clairs are behind it."

"I wasn't sure, until you showed up."

"What does that have to do with it?"

"Well, isn't that why you're here, to do your uncle's dirty work? It's all right, Gabe. Business is business."

Gabe's first inclination was to say that was foolish. But given the St. Clair's past history, he couldn't swear that Buck wasn't involved. He wanted to tell her that he had nothing to do with being there, but Ben and Joey wanted to keep his real job a secret. He didn't believe that the train would be robbed, but he had to assume that the threat was genuine.

He'd never expected her to believe that the threat came from the St. Clairs.

He never expected the law to believe the threat came from Jessie.

"You don't really think I'd do something like that to you, do you, Jessie?"

"Why wouldn't I? You've done worse on your family's behalf."

Suddenly, time flew backward. It was a late fall afternoon when the University of Georgia campus was sprinkled with yellow and orange leaves. Halloween pumpkins peered from the windows of the dormitories, and ghosts made of bedsheets floated in the breeze.

Jessie was in her dorm room sitting at the tiny desk by the window, trying to study, when all she really wanted to do was be back on the mountain where she could take off her shoes and run to the lake to meet Gabe. But Gabe wasn't there. He hadn't been there for four years. He would never be there again. Nothing was the same now. She was a freshmen in college, the first James to go, and she was determined to do well.

Maybe, if she graduated and learned to be like the smart, beautiful girls she'd seen walking around on campus, maybe Gabe would come home and—

No, she wouldn't let herself think that. She didn't even know for sure where Gabe was. Some kind of injury had cut him from the Dolphin team. Could be permanent, the sportscasters had said. He might even be married; she'd seen his picture in a magazine. He'd been with a beautiful blonde. But no, somehow she knew inside he was still hers.

Then, as if she'd dreamed him, she looked up, and there was Gabe standing in her open doorway.

"Gabe?" she whispered. "Is that you?"

"Sure thing, Jess. How are you?"

"Fine—now," she answered, and flew into his arms. "I didn't think I'd ever see you again."

"I'm not sure I ought to have come."

That was when her roommate came in, caught sight of Jess and Gabe, and gasped. "Oops. Sorry, didn't know you had company. I'll just get my books and leave. I have to study."

But she didn't leave immediately. She stared, openmouthed, at Gabe and back at Jessie, disbelief written across her face. "Aren't you . . . ?"

"Gabriel St. Clair," Gabe answered easily. "Jessie and I are old friends. Please, don't let me run you out of your room. I was just about to invite Jessie to go for a walk."

"Yes!" Jessie said, and practically dragged Gabe from the room. Having her roommate say more words to Gabe in two minutes than she'd spoken to Jessie in a week was unnerving. It was only later that Jessie had understood the difference Gabe's presence made. Where she'd been a nonperson before, from that day on she would be a force to be reckoned with in Leeds Hall. A subsequent invitation to join the most prestigious sorority on campus came out of the blue. Jessie had turned it down.

For by that time she'd learned that Gabe hadn't come to see her, but to ask her for something, something she would never give.

They'd left the dorm. She watched the other women looking at Gabe with envy, the men recognizing him and turning back to study the woman they'd never noticed before.

Through the lobby and out the door they walked, Gabe holding Jessie's hand as if that was the only thing on his mind.

"I heard you were hurt," she said.

"Yep. Arm injury. Bad news for a wide receiver. Life's a bitch, isn't it?"

"Will you be out long?"

"They don't know yet. Where can we go to talk?"

"Well, there's the student center."

But that didn't work. Too many people recognized the golden god with the golden hands. They stopped to say they remembered watching him play in high school, or college, or ask about the pros.

From the student center they started across the campus toward town.

"I should have asked. Do you have any afternoon classes?"

"No, no more until the morning. How long can you stay?"

"Until tomorrow," he'd said. "Let's get away from here, this is too public."

And without quite knowing how it happened, they had ended up in Gabe's hotel room. Jessie hadn't known that she'd feel awkward, until she heard Gabe close the door.

"Now, Jessie, we can be alone," he said with a smile of relief.

"I suppose. But it seems strange, doesn't it? Being alone together in a hotel room."

He looked at her, and she knew he was seeing Jessie for the first time. His gaze took in her long denim-encased legs and the skin that had turned satiny to the touch. He'd always seen her as a child. Suddenly, in Gabe's eyes, she was a woman, and he was struck by the potency of her gaze.

"You're right, Jess, we've never been together inside like this, have we?" His voice was husky, deeper than it had been before. "I feel like I ought to take off my pants and my shoes and jump in the lake so you won't see what you're doing to me."

"Yes, well, we don't have a lake now, do we? And I want to know what I do to you. I've missed you, Gabe. It's been a long time since we've been . . . together."

They were both remembering that last night before he'd gone away to college, when he'd kissed her, when she'd welcomed his kisses.

"Dammit, Jess, I'm sorry about that night. I never should have kissed you like that. I was just a big horny kid who didn't know better."

"Oh, I understood that. For four years I've thought about you and Laura and how much better she must have been than me."

"No. Dammit, that's not what I meant. She could never hold a candle to you. You were . . . special."

"Am I still, Gabe? I mean there must have been many women willing to comfort you when you were hurt."

"Not so many," he said in a tight voice as

he dropped down to the bed and switched on the light.

"Coming here was a mistake. I never should have done it. I wouldn't have if I hadn't been so . . ." He looked at her, and his voice dropped off. "I've missed you, Jess."

"I've missed you too," she said. "I haven't had anyone to talk to since you left." Jessie thought his smile wavered, then turned into one of regret. She walked toward the window and peered out into the street below.

He came to his feet, almost reaching out for her, then sank back to the bed. "But everything has changed. You've grown up and found a way to get off that mountain. You're a beautiful woman now, not the skinny kid with the long braids who wishes on the first star she sees every night."

"But I am, and my wish is finally coming true."

"Hell!" he swore, and framed the pillow.

"Gabe, what's wrong?" Instantly, she was kneeling beside him, pressing her body between his legs and laying her head against his chest. He was in trouble, and he'd come to her. That was all she needed to hear. "Whatever it is, it will be fine. I'm sure of it. All we have to do is figure it out."

"You don't understand, Jess. All my life I've tried to get away, be somebody, and I thought I'd found a way. Now, it's gone. Everything is lost."

"You haven't lost me, Gabe. I'll always be here for you."

And she was kissing him, caressing him, taking off his clothes. This time she gave him the love of a woman. And there'd been no turning back. They were both adults, both lonely, and he was taking, touching, turning her comfort into a fiery energy that carried them to a place neither had been before.

Afterward, she lay in his arms, feeling as if they'd reached the mountaintop and were looking down at the world.

"Oh, Gabe," she'd whispered, "I've waited for you, for this. Why did it take you so long to come back?"

She felt him grow suddenly still, tense, as he had been the night they'd decided to steal apples from old man Pendleton's prize orchard, and they'd heard someone approaching.

Then he groaned and, untangling her legs from his, sat up, running his fingers through his hair. "I can't believe that I did this, Jess. God, I'm sorry. I didn't come here to seduce you, or to make false promises. All I wanted was your signature on the easement papers. Now—"

Having old man Pendleton catch them would never have turned her so cold as the words she'd just heard. Gabe hadn't come to see her. He didn't want her; all he wanted was her signature on a legal document, the same document the St. Clairs had harassed her to sign for over a year.

She got up and began to dress, trying not to cry, trying to harness the fury that was building inside. "Gabe, if you'd told me why you were here, I might have signed. Did you think you had to make love to me to get what you wanted?"

"No, of course not. That just happened."

"And suppose I sign, what happens to us then?"

"I hadn't thought. I'll take the document back to my uncle. I will have fulfilled my obligations to my family once and for all. Maybe then they'll let me go."

She fastened her jeans and thrust her feet in her running shoes. "What, they're holding you hostage? You can't get away without buying your freedom?"

"Something like that," he'd admitted miserably.

"Well, I won't make it easy for you, Gabe," she said, growing more hurt and angry by the minute. She picked up the briefcase on the desk and stared at it. "You can take this paper back to your uncle and tell him that I won't sign it now, or next month, or next year." Her voice rose until she was practically screaming. "That piece of land can stay landlocked forever. I never want to see you, or your uncle, or your uncle's attorney, again. Thanks for an interesting afternoon."

"No, Jess, wait. I never meant to hurt you. You know I care about you. I always have."

"I don't want to hear it, Gabe," she said, flinging the case at him as she ran from the room. "I don't believe you anymore." He hadn't even stopped the case from hitting his cheek. And he had never come back to face Jessie again.

Until now.

To her credit, she didn't say, *You made love to me to get what you wanted the last time we met*, but the words hung there in the air, as heavy as a balloon almost empty of helium.

"I'm sorry about that, Jessie, more than you'll ever know," he said slowly. "I'm ashamed that I'd let myself be used by my family. But I'm more ashamed that I didn't tell you the truth. I did care about you. I guess I always have."

"You should be ashamed, Gabriel St. Clair. You see, I know you cared about me. Unless you were showing off before your friends, you never lied to me. If a thing was true, you admitted it. Nobody was ever honest with me the way you were. That's why it hurt so much."

"When they cut me from the team, I guess I went a little crazy. I was hurting so bad. Nobody understood. Then I saw you, and everything was all right again until you ran away. You wouldn't listen to what I'd come to say."

"I listened, Gabe. We'd just made love. Me,

for the first time in my life. I lay in your arms, waiting to hear you say, 'I love you, Jess.' "

"And then what would have happened? We would have gotten married and lived on the mountain just like our families, neither of us qualified to do a damned thing. I acted like a heel, Jessie, a first-class heel, but even then I knew that marrying you would have been worse."

"I know that now. But at the time, Gabe, I was still living in the past. I'd waited for you to come back and suddenly you were there, needing me. But all I heard was about how your family wanted my signature on a piece of paper granting them an easement across the only piece of James land they didn't already own. They could have sent anyone else, Gabe. But you were the one who asked. You, who knew what that land meant to me."

"You might as well hear the rest, Jessie. I didn't want to come, but I let my uncle coerce me, or maybe 'bribe' is a better word. The family was draining me dry, both my bank account and my self-confidence. I had no career, no degree, and no future. I had to find another way to buy a whole new dream. Uncle Buck promised if I would only talk to you, it would be the last thing they'd ever ask of me, and they swore they'd never bother you again. I thought that since you'd gone away to school, you wouldn't be so attached to that land. Maybe I was so desperate to get away that I believed them."

"Well, you were wrong. But I don't give up either. Before I'm done, I will have my family's land back. And since this is my building and you're here uninvited, I want you to go."

"Jess, don't do this. Even if you don't want to talk about us, we need to talk about the gold. I have to make arrangements for a horse and camping equipment. Since I'm riding shotgun, it's your responsibility to share the plans you've made."

Jessie sighed. "All right, then. I'll talk to you on Monday."

"Monday? Why not tomorrow? Isn't the saloon closed on Sunday?"

"Yes, but on Sunday I go to church."

"All day?"

"No, afterward I have lunch, and then I go riding on the mountain."

"Fine. We'll have lunch and go riding."

"But you don't have a horse."

"Oh, but I do. I said I'd have to make arrangements. I still have Blaze."

"Where?"

"My cousin Walter keeps him."

"But I didn't think you spoke to any of your family. Why would Walter keep your horse?"

"Let's just say that he's paying off a debt."

Jessie sighed. "All right then. Tomorrow, Gabe. I'll talk to you tomorrow."

"Fine. I'll pick you up after church."

Jessie didn't have the strength to argue. If she didn't get away from the intensity of Gabe's presence, she was going to lose her tenuous hold on her emotions. Keeping up the pretense of strength and indifference was more difficult than she'd thought.

"Conversation only, Gabe. I'm no lovesick teenager wearing her heart on her sleeve for the world to laugh at."

Laugh at? Jessie was right. Gabe had never given her the respect she deserved, always kept their friendship a secret. He'd used her. He might not be able to change what had happened, but he'd let the world know that Gabe St. Clair and Jessie James were friends. He owed her that.

Having reached that decision, he started across the roof, stopped, and turned back. "You're definitely no teenager, and Jane was right. You flap your wings nicely. I can't wait until you get to the doodling." He turned and walked down the stairs at the side of the building, taking them two at a time.

Weakly, Jessie made her way to the railing and looked into the street below. What in God's name was he talking about? Wings? Doodling?

What was she thinking about, agreeing to go

with him to the mountain when she ought to be concentrating on arranging to be away from the saloon?

Still, the lilt in Gabe's step was back. They'd met and talked, and she'd given him every opportunity to leave. He hadn't. She let out a deep breath and allowed herself a tiny smile of hope. She hadn't been the one to call in the holdup threat. But whoever did had succeeded where everything else had failed.

Gabriel St. Clair had come home again.

She saw the light come on in his room across the way, silhouetting him through the window as he unzipped his jeans and let them slide down his legs. As if he knew she was watching, he blew her a kiss and switched off the light.

Gabriel St. Clair was no angel. Jessie James knew better than anyone that he was a wicked man.

He brought back wicked memories.

And stirred wicked longings.

And he knew exactly what he was doing.

The next morning Gabe woke up early. He dressed in the only dress shirt he had, picked up his sport coat, and headed for the dining room, catching Lonnie by surprise when he asked, "Do you have a tie I could borrow?"

"Sure, you going somewhere?"

"Thought I might go to church."

Lonnie unfastened the tie he was wearing and handed it to Gabe.

"I'd try the little Methodist church out Pumpkinvine Road," Jane said with a knowing smile.

Gabe tied the bright pink silk creation around his neck and grinned. He was wearing a blue shirt and a neon-pink tie; there was no way he'd slip into church without being seen.

"Those services run pretty long," Jane said as she filled his cup with coffee. "You'll probably be hungry when you get out. Want me to fix you a picnic basket for afterward?"

"Why not? Yes, Jane, I'd like that very much." He glanced around. The small dining room was filling up. "I hope it won't be too much trouble."

"No trouble at all. I have a cooler. There's some leftover fried chicken and some cherry pie. I'll manage."

"Fried chicken," he said, and grinned. "Perfect!"

The church was just as he'd remembered, perched on the side of the mountain, its windows wide open, the air filled with the sound of voices. He couldn't say that he'd spent much time in church as a boy. The St. Clairs were never devout, but if they had been, they would have been Baptists.

Gabe parked his Jeep under a stand of pines and started inside. Just as he'd suspected, as he walked down the aisle and sat down in the front row, every eye in the sanctuary was focused on him, including those belonging to a dark-haired member of the choir, wearing a red robe.

He inclined his head, gave her a big wink, and took hold of the hymnal being offered by a lady beside him. He joined in the singing with enthusiasm. He didn't know when he'd felt so good.

The church was hot, very hot, and his sport coat was a wool blend. By the time they'd had a prayer, passed the collection plate, listened to the Scripture and a sermon on trust and repentance that hit uncomfortably close to home, the perspiration was rolling down Gabe's face and dripping on Lonnie's tie.

Gabe never took his eyes off Jessie's face. She hadn't been lying when she said she was going to church. She actually sang in the choir. He shouldn't be surprised; after all, he'd heard her sing. The services ended with a solo in which Jessie sang about angels and forgiveness.

Behind her, the white-painted brick was flecked with gold. Gabe remembered that many of the bricks and the paint used in the construction of the old buildings were sprinkled with gold dust.

There was something almost spiritual about Jessie standing there beneath the stained-glass window, backed by a wall that was flecked with gold. There was something genuine in the welcome expressed by the minister and the congregation as Gabe left the church afterward.

Since he was at the front of the church, he was one of the last to leave. Several of the members were people he'd known, and they didn't seem surprised to see him. Finally, as he reached the last row, an old man stood and stepped out into the aisle, blocking his exit.

"Heard you were in town, boy."

"Uncle Buck? What in h-heaven's name are you doing here?"

"I attend services here, now and again. I might ask you the same question."

He answered honestly, "I came to see Jessie."

"It's about time," Buck said, gave a nod to someone behind Gabe, and walked slowly out the door, leaving Gabe openmouthed and speechless.

The person Buck had nodded to wasn't speechless. Jessie was removing her robe as she touched Gabe on the shoulder, demanding, "What are you doing here, and where in God's name did you get that tie?"

"Why, Miss James, such language. This tie is a divine creation. I believe it goes very well with your . . . shorts?"

Jessie looked down at her bare legs and quickly redressed in her choir robe. "It's hot," she said lamely. "And we wear our robes home."

She was wearing a pair of white shorts and a red-and-white gingham shirt tied at the waist. The running shoes had been exchanged for a pair of red sandals with little bows.

"Get in the Jeep, Jess," he ordered, allowing his amusement to show. "Quick, or I'm going to pick you up and put you there. Now!"

She must have believed him, for she scrambled into the Jeep and slammed the door.

"I don't know why you're doing this, Gabe. You must know how foolish this looks."

"I've come to fetch you as I said I would. Where would you like to eat?"

FOUR

"When did Uncle Buck become a Methodist?"

"When he started calling on the organist, Effie Stevens," Jessie answered.

"Uncle Buck is sweet on your organist? That's hard to believe. Almost as hard to believe as his approval of you."

"Your uncle always approved of me, Gabe. Otherwise, he'd have stopped our roaming the mountain together. Why else do you think he sent you to ask for the easement?"

Gabe didn't answer. Instead, he turned on the radio, found a country station, and let the music catch in the wind and be drawn out the open windows.

There was something about the clean mountain air that could be found no place else on earth.

If Jessie really wanted to make it big, she ought to find some way to bottle and sell it.

"When did you start singing, Jess?"

"I always sang when I was alone."

"But not around me?"

"I didn't know what you'd say, and I was afraid you'd laugh at me."

"Did I ever laugh at you?"

She didn't trust herself to look at him. Her eyes were still full of the picture of him standing there in the sunshine, his blue shirt the same color of his eyes and his sun-streaked hair glittering like fool's gold in the light. There was something powerful about Gabriel, something that transcended the normal and spilled straight over into one of her most secret fantasies.

Some women, she supposed, preferred dark, sinister men with secrets and raging passion that only the right lover could tame. But Gabe's sexual pull was different; it was the power of a rushing mountain stream that hit the jagged rocks and smoothed them with its force. Its appeal was in its simplicity, the illusion of calm, the promise of the undercurrent hidden below. That hadn't changed.

"No, you never laughed at me. I just expected that you would. And it was important that you didn't."

"But I pretended that you weren't important

to me, and that was wrong. I let a bunch of shallow people treat you badly. I should have stood up for you."

"I understood what you were doing. I never blamed you, Gabe. You wanted to be somebody, and suddenly you were. To me, you always were."

"I guess," Gabe said slowly, trying to give voice to feelings he'd never allowed himself to examine before, "I guess you fed my dreams in a way nobody else did."

"That's nice, that's probably a good beginning for a song, if I think about it. Tell me what it means."

"I knew there was something wrong with my family, but I thought it was because my grandfather had been a prisoner of war. When he came home, he was a hero, but the world never knew that he wasn't quite right. He had turned into a mean, vicious old man. They said my grandmother was an angel. She never complained about looking after him, but she got quieter and quieter.

"Then there was the poker game," he explained, "where Grandpa won the James mine. For a while things got better—until the mine played out. After that the bad luck started, bad luck the St. Clairs caused."

"How?"

"Well, I remember once that the car stopped

running in the middle of winter. Without it, Dad lost his job."

"That wasn't his fault, was it?"

"It was. All he had to do was make sure the car had antifreeze. He didn't. It froze and cracked the block. There were always things like that happening, things that could have been prevented. The only really responsible St. Clair was apparently my grandmother. If she'd lived, things might have been different. But after Grandpa Evan died, they said she died of a broken heart."

"But they were proud of you. I remember your daddy watching you play football, laughing when you scored."

"Yeah, but it was probably because he'd bet on the game, and he was counting his winnings."

Jessie didn't respond to the bitterness in Gabe's voice. The St. Clairs were always considered ne'er-do-wells, but she'd charged it off to ignorance and bad luck. She'd understood how much Gabe had hated it. She understood about Gabe's father, too, because she'd seen her father react in almost the same way.

"You're right. I wanted to be somebody," Gabe went on, "do something, find out about the world beyond the mountain. Football was to be my way out."

"I know. I used to listen to you talk, and I could see that world. I wanted you to go, to find your dream. But I knew that meant leaving me behind."

"Nobody else cared, Jessie, except you. I guess I never told you how much that meant to me."

"So you became a big college athlete who was drafted by the pros. Was it what you thought, Gabe?"

"For a time. The Miami Dolphins gave me a bonus to leave college early and sign to play football with them, and I thought I was on my way. Then I got hurt, and there was no Jessie to share my uncertainties."

"Was that when you came back home?"

"Yes, when the team doctor said I could never play again. My father and my uncle offered me my own piece of land if I'd stay and share my injury insurance money."

"What made you leave?"

"In a weird kind of way it was you. The piece of land they offered me was part of that landlocked section that belonged to my grandmother. It was the one they wanted to sell when you refused to allow the easement."

"I didn't know it was to be your land, Gabe."

"They were using me, Jess. After I realized what I'd done, I was so angry that I never even told them that I'd seen you. I never went back. I used most of my injury insurance money to go to college and get a job."

"Then I guess I'm glad about what happened. Because if you had come back, I probably would never have gotten angry enough to change my life either. So, you're forgiven, Gabe. You're right, it's time we put it behind us."

He wanted to say something, something that would let her know that she'd done it again, listened to his uncertainties and made them seem unimportant. He'd revealed more about his life to her in the last half hour than he'd ever done before with anyone. Jessie had a way of destroying his demons.

In the warm afternoon sunlight, with the wind whipping his hair, it didn't feel as if ten years had passed. It felt as if he was eighteen again. Except this time, Jessie was eighteen, too, and they no longer had to answer to anybody but themselves.

He swore mentally. That line of reasoning wasn't going to work. They weren't going to the lake for a swim. They weren't going to build a campfire, or sit on the dock and talk. He was thirty-two years old now. With an effort he brought his thoughts back to the present, and with a voice reasonably light, he asked, "And do you write all the songs for your group yourself?"

"Some of them. Sometimes, when the band is fooling around, we try out new things."

"You're very good."

"No, I just try to make the audience feel what I feel."

And she'd been told that she did it well. But she wasn't singing now, and she hoped that Gabe couldn't feel the tension she kept tamped down, the indecision she'd managed to conquer. Deep inside she was still the same Jessie who dared the devil to mess with her and wished on the first star each night.

Life was a kick in the teeth, she thought. She'd always believed that Gabe would come back. She'd trusted him to find what he wanted and return for her.

The first time he'd come back to her, she'd been caught by surprise and her own foolish pride. This time she wouldn't allow herself to be fooled. He was there for a reason. All that nonsense about someone holding up the gold train had to be pure St. Clair fiction.

Gabe took the mountain curves on two wheels, spraying gravel into the dense forest on either side, letting out the kind of hell-raising yell that had once been the familiar cry of his youth.

Too late, she wondered about their destination. "Where are we going, Gabe?"

"I thought we'd stop at Walter's and make sure that Blaze is ready for a long ride. We'll see if he has an extra horse for you. You did say you rode on Sunday afternoon, didn't you?"

"Our farm?" Her words stuck in her throat.

Gabe heard the tension in her voice and slowed the vehicle so that he could reassure her. "We won't, if you'd rather not. We can drive up to the lake instead."

"No! I'd rather not go to the lake. The farm is fine. It's just that I've been away a long time."

He knew exactly how long it had been. He'd given Walter the down payment on the land from his bonus money. Jessie would have been a senior in high school then.

"It must have been hard for you, having your father sell your home."

"It was hard. I was glad that Pop didn't live to see it. Suddenly, we had to move into an apartment in town. I don't think Daddy ever got used to living there. But it helped me understand how trapped you used to feel before you left."

"Are you sure about the farm? We can just have a picnic and forget riding."

"No, it's time I faced it. And—it will be easier with you."

Moments later they turned off onto a narrow, rutted road that angled back down the mountain. They crossed Pumpkinvine Creek on a bridge that seemed much shakier than Jessie remembered. Then the house was there, nestled among a stand of spruce trees overlooking the barn and the miniature valley below where Walter had planted tobacco and apple trees.

Jessie felt an odd strangling sensation in her chest. She didn't remember the house looking so small. Its paint was mildewed and flaking. The tin roof was rusty, and the porch was noticeably sagging.

"It looks so sad," she said, as Gabe drove up to the door and came to a stop. "It used to be such a happy place."

Gabe studied the house critically. He could tell that it looked very different from the way it had when Jessie lived there. Her aunt's flower beds and vegetable garden had long been overrun by weeds. It was obvious that Walter and his young wife hadn't been any more interested in keeping them up than Jessie's grandfather and her father had been.

A woman appeared in the doorway, a baby slung across her hip. Her stretch pants had a tear in the knee, and there was a stain of what looked like baby food on her shirt.

"Yes? May I help you?"

Gabe swung his feet to the ground and walked toward the porch. "I'm Gabe St. Clair. Is Walter here?"

"He's down in the barn, working on the tractor. Go on down."

Gabe turned back to the Jeep, waiting for

Jessie to join him. She seemed reluctant to get out. "Coming?"

"No, I think I'll just wait for you," she said.

"You can sit on the porch," the woman called out. "It's cooler up here. And I'd love the company."

As Jessie climbed out, Gabe made his way to the barn. He was uncomfortable about leaving her, yet he didn't know what else to do. She wasn't having any easier time coming home to the farm than he was facing his family.

"Walt?"

"In here. If you know anything about tractors, you're welcome."

The barn was shady and still. Bees buzzed, doing loop-de-loops in the rays of sunlight that streamed through the nail holes in the tin roof. Dust from the hay hovered in the air, and the smell of horses was strong. Bending over the engine of the tractor was the cousin Gabe had corresponded with monthly but hadn't seen in years.

"I don't, but I'll be glad to have a look."

Walter raised up. "Gabe? I don't believe it. Didn't you get that final payment on my loan?"

"I got it. That isn't why I'm here."

"If it's about Blaze, don't worry. He's welcome to stay as long as I do. For an old man he's in good shape. I still ride him, like I promised."

Gabe looked down at the engine, taking in

the dirt and the grease that leaked on the floor. "What's wrong?"

"The whole thing ought to be junked. But people have stopped smoking, and with the price of tobacco in the toilet, I can't afford to replace it."

"Bad, huh?"

"You wouldn't like to buy a farm, would you?"

"No thanks. I managed to get out of here once—I sure don't want any part of coming back."

"You were the smart one, Gabe. The rest of us finally figured that out. Uncle Buck is the only one still up the mountain, and I'm thinking he's ready to come into town."

Gabe didn't know what to say to that. The idea that Buck would even consider moving to town was pure sacrilege. "That surprises me almost as much as seeing him in church this morning."

"Yeah, it's amazing what the right woman can do for a man, even one as cantankerous as Uncle Buck." Walter leaned back and wiped his face with the rag he was holding. "What brings you here, Gabe?"

"I'm making the wagon ride to Atlanta with the gold train. I'd like to ride Blaze, and I came to check him out."

"He's in the corral behind the barn, and your saddle is hanging on the wall."

"Don't suppose you have another horse around, do you?"

"Nope. Why?"

"Jessie's with me. I thought we'd go riding."

"Well, I reckon Blaze will carry you both, if the lady's willing."

"I think I'll just say hello to the old boy first, then I'll check it out with Jessie."

"Sure thing. I'd better get back to this piece of junk."

Gabe left Walter with his head over the tractor. Jessie was right. There was definitely something sad about the farm, even if there was nothing sad about the big black horse when he caught sight of Gabe. Ten years might have made Gabe a stranger in town, but not to the horse who'd grown up with the boy.

Jessie climbed the steps to the porch, trying not to let her dismay show.

"I'm Rachel St. Clair, Walter's wife. You're Jessie James, aren't you?"

"Yes. Have we met?"

"No. I'm from over in Shady Grove. But I've seen you in town. Walter told me how you and Gabe used to tear across this mountain before he left. You getting back together?"

There was something unmistakably wistful about Rachel's voice. The baby began to fret, and Rachel let out a sigh. "It's just too hot for

October. Even the people who used to come up here to escape the heat don't come anymore. Nobody comes up here. I wish—"

"It's hot in town too. All those people just seem to take up all the air. Up here, it seems to go on forever."

"Well, you can have it. Me and Walter are thinking about selling out and moving over to Tennessee. They're hiring at that new automobile company, and Walter thinks he can get on."

"Sell the farm?"

"If we can find anybody to buy it. Walter's been asking around."

Jessie felt suddenly faint. He couldn't sell the farm, not until she could buy it back. She sat down with a lurch and leaned forward, allowing her head to drop between her knees.

"You all right? Let me get you a glass of ice water. I'll be right back."

The screen door slammed behind her, and Jessie could hear her headed for the kitchen. Slowly, Jessie raised her head and looked around, seeing the farm with the eyes of someone who'd never seen it before. It was run-down, it was neglected, but it was home, and her heart hurt to think nobody wanted it now.

How could that be? A farm was the promise of the future. It was the reflection of the past.

⟡————————⟡

Jessie was finishing a glass of ice-cold pure mountain water when Gabe and his cousin Walter came walking to the house. They were both laughing, and that laughter sounded good.

"Where's Blaze?" she asked.

"He's in the corral, complaining that he isn't going on a picnic," Gabe answered. "It's too hot for him to carry both of us and a picnic basket. Guess we're going to have to postpone our ride."

"Fine," she said too eagerly. "I've got to be getting back to town anyway. Thank you for the water, Rachel," she said, "and I'll be back in touch about the farm."

Moments later they were driving back up the mountain, Jessie deep in her own thoughts, and Gabriel waiting for her to share them.

"What about having lunch on the creek bank?" he said finally.

Jessie looked around. They were almost back at the creek. She was having trouble assimilating what he'd said. "I don't think there's a good place to park along here," she finally said.

Gabe grinned. "Oh, but there is. At least I think it's probably still here."

He crossed over the bridge and turned up the mountain, driving slowly until he found the place he was looking for, then left the highway, brushing through the mountain laurel to a spot by the creek completely hidden from the road. He cut off the engine and turned toward Jessie with a smile. "See, what did I tell you?"

"I guess you must have come here a lot." *But not with me.*

"I spent some time here, yes." He leaned his head back against the seat and closed his eyes. Suddenly, he was in high school again, the girl sitting beside him was Laura, and he'd wanted her so bad that he hurt.

"Laura?" Jessie said softly.

"Yes. We'd come here and—"

"Make love?"

"I don't know that you'd call it that. Laura was the kind of girl who said yes one minute and no the next. She drove me totally crazy."

"You mean you never—"

"No, I never. For a jock I was embarrassingly inexperienced. You know the funny thing? I look back on those days and think that she would have let me, but I wasn't smart enough to know it. Instead, I walked around in torment all the time. If I hadn't had you to talk with, Jessie, I would probably have taken drugs or been in jail somewhere."

Jessie didn't want to hear about Gabe and Laura. She'd listened to him back then, and though she hadn't understood what he was going through, she'd tried. Sex to a guy appeared to be a physical release, nothing more. It didn't seem to have a thing to do with love.

"I'm glad I could help. Too bad I didn't have anybody who understood what I was going through."

Gabe opened his eyes and sat up. He'd never thought that Jessie might have problems. He never saw Jessie as an equal at all, not until that last week before he'd left for college when everything changed.

"Oh, Jess, I'm sorry. You should have said something."

"What should I have said, Gabe? That my body was changing too? That I was feeling strange things, that I wanted to touch you and wanted you to touch me?"

"You felt that way about me?" He'd known she had a crush on him, but he'd always thought of her as a little sister. He was becoming a man, and his feelings were different.

"Is that so hard to understand? You were the best-looking guy in school, the prize catch, and you were mine. You were mine before you ever belonged to Laura. And I hated her for being older, for being stupid, for being where I wanted to be and never would.

"But most of all, Gabe, I hated you for not knowing what you had in me."

And suddenly all the frustration came back. Jessie jerked open the car door and plunged through the laurel toward the creek. She didn't know what she was doing, admitting to Gabe that she'd lusted after him. She didn't know why he was telling her all his private thoughts again. Once she'd hurt with him when she'd listened, and now he was doing it again and she was letting him. But this time, she had her own hurt to deal with.

"I'm sorry, Jessie." Gabe caught up with her, took her shoulder, and turned her around. "You were always there for me, the only one I could talk to, the only real friend I had. I'm sorry I was so selfish."

"Don't, Gabe. That's what friends are for. It wasn't your fault that I wanted more. I could never compete with the town girls. I've always been the ugly duckling."

Gabe's fingers tightened on Jessie's shoulder. His breath quickened, and the blue of his eyes deepened. "Oh, Jessie, don't you know how very beautiful you are?"

She didn't. He could tell that she didn't believe the truth. She had no idea how desirable she was, standing there with the sunlight dappling hair so dark that it looked like the lake on a summer afternoon flecked with the reflection of the sun. Her lips full and parted in invitation. Her brown eyes fired with wanting.

"You were never an ugly duckling. You were Jessie, and I always knew you were mine."

"But you never wanted me, Gabe," she whispered.

"I was a fool. I probably still am."

"No, Gabe. You know exactly what you're doing. I think you always did. Just like this drive. You didn't bring me up here to talk about gold. We could have done that back in town. Why did you kidnap me at the church?"

"Because I wanted to spend some time with you. I'm as uncertain about where we're going as you are, Jessie. But I'd like us to take a chance and find out. Is that possible?"

"I don't think so, Gabe. We're both suffering from an overdose of memories and feelings that were left unresolved. We're still carrying all that emotion around with us."

She was right. It was time to change the subject. "Maybe. What I am sure of is that I'm hungry. We've got our schedule reversed. We're supposed to eat, then talk. You find us a spot while I get the food."

Moments later he was spreading an old army blanket on the ground beside the creek. He opened the cooler, looked at Jessie, and grinned.

"What are you smiling about, Gabriel St. Clair? Did you forget the food?"

"Oh, no. There's bread for the body, wine

for the spirit, and a few foods for the soul. Let's eat, and afterward I'm going to tell you all about mating customs of the New Guinea flapdoodle hen."

They ate the food and talked about safe things, music, her saloon—even discussing the gold was suddenly safer than the past. Finally, Gabe gathered up the remains of the picnic and repacked the cooler, returning it to the Jeep. When he came back, she was lying on the blanket with her arms folded beneath her head.

Gabe would never understand why Jessie thought she was an ugly duckling. Just looking at her now made his pulse quicken, and the thoughts he was thinking were certainly not the kind he used to have. He lay down beside her, as far away as possible, forcing himself to go slow.

"Do you still like jelly beans?" he asked.

"Sure. Do you still like tacos?"

He loved her voice, low and a bit gravelly.

"Yep, the hotter, the better."

"When are you going to tell me about the guinea hen?" she asked, turning to her side and leaning on one elbow.

She was too close. He groaned silently. "Maybe I'll save that for another time."

"Another time?" she repeated, as if she didn't believe there would be one. Then he kissed her. She hadn't expected it. He hadn't meant to do it. They'd spent several hours avoiding any subject that might bring back memories, and then, in one second, all that was gone. There was nothing but the beat of her heart and roar of blood pulsing through her veins as she fell back to the blanket and he followed, never relinquishing her lips.

For Jessie, every touch was magnified. The blanket pressing against her back seemed to mold itself to her. Gabe's hair felt like skeins of silk between her fingers. His lips smudged her skin with heated imprints. He was murmuring words that she couldn't understand, saying things she sensed but did not hear.

At last.

He rolled her over, lifting her on top, pulling her face down so that he could nibble at her lips. Her hands clenched into fists between them, then loosened and played across his chest, outlining the strong plains and valleys. "What's this, Gabe?"

Her finger was tracing a fresh scar between his nipple and his shoulder.

"It's nothing," he said casually, wincing as she applied pressure.

"Looks like a bullet wound to me," she said,

running her tongue across his chest. "What kind of work do you do for the governor?"

"This and that, whatever he assigns me to."

She lifted her eyebrow to show her disbelief, then planted a kiss on the scar. "I think you're the outlaw, Gabriel St. Clair, not me. You know I always have a spot in my gang for a good man."

"What makes you think I'm good?" he said playfully, simply holding her and watching the expressions ripple across her face.

"I'm Jessie James." She laughed. "And I always recognize one of my own kind. Want to ride with me?"

Somebody laughed. It couldn't be him. Gabe was no longer the wild mountain kid he'd once been.

Somebody moaned. It couldn't be her. She never allowed her personal feelings to pour out.

They rolled again, off the blanket, Jessie's bottom pressed against the pine straw, her head arched back, her legs parted to take his weight between them.

Gabe, looking down at her, took in the flush that colored her cheeks, lips swollen from his kisses, and eyes meeting his without guile or apology.

Somewhere in the chaos of his mind he knew that this was crazy. This was trouble. This was letting loose demons he'd worked too hard to control before he knew where they were going. Somehow he forced himself to stop and roll away.

For a long time they lay still, stunned, disbelieving.

Neither spoke. Neither knew what to say.

Finally, Jessie cleared her throat. "I—I don't suppose you'd go away and forget this ever happened, would you?"

"Believe me, Jess, I wish I could."

"Why did you stop? I would have let you make love to me. You knew it."

Gabe took her hand. "Yes, I knew. And God knows, I wanted to, but we've already gone down that road, and it ended in disaster. This time we can't let ourselves be carried away because of some overpowering passion."

"Is that what you think we're feeling?"

He wasn't certain he wanted to answer. He wasn't certain he knew the answer. "I don't know. I wonder what would have happened if our lives had been different, if I hadn't been hurt, if I hadn't made love to you that day, if I hadn't left the mountain?"

"Oh, no. Don't go feeling regrets now, Gabriel St. Clair. I'm not taking the responsibility for your failures. They're yours, just as mine belong to me."

She jerked her hand away and got to her feet. "It's late, Gabe. I have to get back to the Gold Dust. I need to think about—a lot of things."

❖―――――❖

Back at the hotel, Gabe stopped the car. Jessie started to open the door, felt Gabe's hand on her arm, and stopped.

"Where does this leave us, Jessie?"

"Just where we were when you came. No-where." Jessie let out a deep breath. "We deliver the gold. Then you go back to your life, and I'll stay in mine."

"I'm not sure I want to do that."

"Don't make this into more than it was, Gabe. If you can't handle the wagon train, send someone else. That way neither of us has to worry about what might happen."

"I think I'm more worried that it won't happen," he said softly.

"I'm talking about the holdup," Jessie said, and climbed out of the Jeep. She walked around to the driver's side and stopped to look at Gabe. This time they were both hurting. They'd once been best friends. Then they'd been lovers. They weren't either now, and she didn't know where they'd go from here.

"Thank you, Gabe," she said softly, "for being with me when I went back to the farm. About the future, I've stopped planning. I take it as it comes."

As he drove away, he pressed the gas pedal too

hard, then hit the brakes hard, setting off a squeal that caught the attention of his cousin, the sheriff, who pointed a finger in mock warning. Making a U-turn, Gabe drove back, pulling into a parking space in front of the hotel. For a long time he sat, trying to make some kind of sense out of what had happened.

He thought about failures and taking the responsibilities for them. He thought about regret and blame. He thought about the mother who'd left him when he was eight and the father who might as well have gone, for he was never really there for a boy who needed love. He thought about Pumpkinvine Mountain and Jessie.

He wondered if he was going to be sorry he'd come home.

FIVE

Gabe hadn't fooled Jessie for a minute. That had been a bullet hole, a recent bullet hole. He'd been wounded by someone who'd intended to do permanent damage. He might say he worked for the governor, but suppose that was a lie? Suppose he really was there to steal the gold?

Nobody held up a wagon train in the nineties. That was something out of the Old West. Sure, they had drugs and crime in Dahlonega, but this was absurd.

Gabriel St. Clair having a bullet wound was even more absurd. She didn't know how Gabe made his living, but he was no crook. Whatever had brought him back, the sheriff seemed to be a part of it. She couldn't imagine that the sheriff would be a party to a crime. But he was a St. Clair, and that changed all the rules. Still, the whole idea was bizarre. She'd been grasping at straws when she'd accused Gabe of making love to her because he thought that would get him the gold. That hadn't made sense to her then, and it didn't now.

But the bullet wound was a fact. And so was the note she found shoved under her door when she got back. *He isn't what he seems. Beware!* She read it in shock.

Gabe had been gone for ten years. He'd spent three years in college, one playing professional ball, then he'd dropped off the face of the earth. Suppose he'd been in jail? Now, suddenly, just when she was moving Pop's gold out of the bank and into Atlanta, he'd turned up.

The St. Clairs had always stolen from the Jameses. But Gabe only turned up when they wanted something from Jessie. Her mind went around and around, caught between sentiment and fact. There had to be more to this than fourteen ounces of gold. She just couldn't figure out what.

For a while that afternoon she'd allowed herself to relax her guard. But the note jerked her back to reality. She didn't want to believe that Gabe was a thief, but she wasn't so sure that she could trust her instincts. Was she heart-stoppingly, gut wrenchingly, mind-alteringly in love with a thief? She needed time to think, to find answers. She'd start by making sure they weren't alone again together.

But there was one thing she had to do before they left. First thing Monday morning, she'd make a trip to the bank. First she'd ask about a second loan to pay Walter what he'd invested in the farm. Then she'd check out the safety-deposit box one last time.

She didn't want to think about what it would mean sharing a wagon with Gabe for three days. But she couldn't depend on outsiders. The gold was her responsibility, and even if she didn't believe the tip about Gabe, she had to be sure whoever had made it believed that she did.

And she might also find a way to shake Gabe up a little.

On Wednesday morning, at the edge of town, the mules were already being hitched to the wagon. Gabe and the others were waiting for the sheriff and his deputies to arrive with the gold.

"My, my, isn't this exciting," Jane was saying. Dressed in a gingham dress and bonnet, she was sitting on the seat next to Lonnie. "A real Conestoga wagon. I feel like a pioneer."

"That's because you know you don't have to drive these mules," Lonnie complained. "And these boots are hot."

"Oh, the animals are as excited as I am. I had a little talk with the lead mule, Horace, and he told me he has an eye on one of those fillies that pulls a carriage in downtown Atlanta."

Lonnie lifted his eyebrows. "How would he know about a horse in downtown Atlanta? Atlanta is seventy miles away."

"She's a native. They knew each other intimately before she went away. And I promised to see that they have a chance to get reacquainted, unless she's made another commitment," Jane said.

"I thought mules were sterile?" Lonnie questioned.

Jane gave him a 'Don't believe everything you hear' look. "First, Horace is very special. Second, he may be sterile, but he isn't dead."

"If I were you, Jane, I'd keep any conversations you have with the mules quiet. I'm afraid Gabriel is already half-convinced that you're loony."

Jane gave Lonnie a big smile and gave Gabe a long look. "I don't think I have a thing to do with his being turned inside out for the last two days. Whatever is chewing on his feathers isn't me. I think this is a case of the more you can't have a thing, the more you want it."

Jessie, mounted on her horse, was listening to Jane's chatter. She wasn't feeling very well this morning either. She'd had little sleep the last two nights. She'd sworn not to see Gabe, but she hadn't expected him to stay away.

She touched the note in her pocket and wondered if she ought to have taken it to Joey St. Clair, then decided that it was just as well if Gabe didn't know. She sighed, and her tension translated to the horse, who danced nervously away from the wagon.

"You okay, Jess?" Gabe called from the other side of the wagon where he was to ride.

Jessie managed to shake her head in reassurance as she calmed the horse. "Fine."

The other members of the train were driving farm wagons, buggies, even a hay wagon. The only other authentic part of the train was the chuck wagon, stocked with beans, burgers, and steaks. The people who set up the trek were fully prepared to go as authentic as the participants wished.

Finally, they heard the police sirens, marking the arrival of the gold. The sheriff, his deputies, and Gabe had met Jessie at the bank at nine o'clock. They'd opened the safety-deposit box, removed the locked pouch of gold dust and nuggets, and signed the papers transferring the gold from the bank to Jessie and on to the sheriff. Now the sheriff was moving it to the specially built lockbox inside the wagon and handing Jessie the key.

Gabe, watching the procedure, checked his pockets, reassured that a second, matching key rested there. He told himself that it wasn't that he didn't trust Jessie. He did. It was the second warning tip that worried him. It had come that morning according to Joey, who still hadn't identified the original caller. But the new threat was written. *Beware of outlaws. There's a thief in the night.*

Gabe had called Ben, who had reinforced the governor's demand that the gold be protected. Joey decided to send two deputies along. Though he thought it was somebody trying to make trouble, he had no suspects. The James family, except for Jessie, had always been weak. Like the St. Clairs, they'd always managed to make a good thing go wrong. The only thing they'd ever done that Gabriel approved of was produce Jessie.

But, as Joey candidly pointed out, for years the St. Clairs' only claim to legitimacy was Gabe. Some might say that made the families about even.

Jessie gave the signal.

Lonnie flicked the reins.

Horace looked back over his shoulder and dug in.

"Apply your strap, Lonnie," Gabe directed.

"Don't you dare hit Horace," Jane argued.

"Jane," Jessie said quietly but firmly, "mules are stubborn animals. If Lonnie doesn't show them he's in charge, we're going to have a long trip."

"Nonsense," Jane quipped. "Let me speak to the big boy privately." She hopped down from her perch, moved quickly to the mule, whispered in his ear, and returned to her seat. Moments later Horace moved down the road.

Gabe was worried. He'd had every kind of assignment, but this might be the most disturbing. He couldn't get a handle on the thief, if there was one. Official inquiries had turned up no local suspects. Joey had sent the note on to the lab. Gabe wished he could talk to Jessie about the new development, but she seemed withdrawn.

By noon, when they stopped to water the animals and eat a light lunch, he was already stiff, and they'd only covered ten miles. Blaze was holding up well; it was Gabe who was tiring. He wasn't back to full strength physically.

It was late afternoon when they reached the Etowah River, near Silver City, where they'd camp for the night. Gabe had the drivers circle the wagons, as if they were preparing for an Indian attack. He made certain that the horses and mules were watered, rubbed down, and fed from the accompanying hay wagon. Jessie avoided contact with Gabe by overseeing the building of the symbolic campfire and the setting up of the tents and bedrolls.

While the cook was preparing their meal, she checked the locked box, making certain that the thread she'd secretly stretched across the inside of the box was still intact.

The beans and hamburgers were reasonably authentic. The coolers of ice to chill the beer and soft drinks weren't. Jessie continued to avoid Gabe, who seemed to be trying equally hard to avoid her.

Good. That would make the next two days easier. By Saturday they'd be in Atlanta, and the gold would be delivered to the governor. They'd drive the wagons home for the official start of Gold Rush Days, leaving Gabe behind, and life would get back to normal.

Jane and Lonnie were sitting in aluminum chairs. "There are just some comforts that bow to age and ingenuity," she explained, with a twinkle in her eye. "Are we going to sing around the campfire?"

"Yeah," someone called out. "Jessie, you brought your guitar, didn't you?"

"No, I didn't."

"Yes, she did," Lonnie corrected, and drew her case from under the wagon seat.

There was nothing to do but comply. Jessie strummed her pick across the strings, made a couple of adjustments, and began to play. She played songs that the group could join in on, "You Are My Sunshine," "Froggy Went A-courting," "Clementine."

"Play one of your songs, Jessie," Jane said. "My ears would like something sweet and sad before bedtime."

"Oh, I don't think so," Jessie demurred.

"Why not, Jess?" a familiar deep voice said, a voice that wasn't as light as it intended to be. "Let's hear about the one who got away."

It had been inevitable, from the moment the guitar came out. "All right." And she began to sing about the woman inside of her who'd broken free.

> *"And then I saw him once again.*
> *It's the same way now that it was then.*
> *And I love him.*
> *Love him. I still love him*
> *Crazy . . . Crazy."*

When she finished the last word, her throat was so tight that she could barely sing. There was a light smattering of applause, just enough time to allow her to stand and replace the guitar in its case.

Jane followed her lead. "I'm tired. The pioneers must have developed leather bottoms. Good night, folks."

Jessie watched the two octogenarians fold up their chairs and walk side by side toward the tent they'd pitched in the edge of the woods.

She hadn't noticed the two bedrolls that had been unfolded and positioned beneath the wagon. One was hers, the other—"Now just a minute, Gabe. You aren't sleeping here."

"Of course I am, Jess. How can we guard the gold from a distance?"

"But—but—" He was right. The gold pouch was locked in the wagon, and she had to stay close. If Gabe was going to play out his role of protector, he, too, had to stay close. At least this way neither of them could make off with the pouch without the other knowing it.

"What do you say, Jessie?" he said softly. "I don't like what's happening. I think we both need a good night's sleep. Let's call a truce, for the duration of the trek."

"Can we do that?"

"We can try." She agreed. But going to sleep was not so simple. The wagons were far enough apart that there was privacy, but close enough so that you weren't alone. Aside from that, the sheriff's men were stationed at both sides of the camp.

Jessie lay on her sleeping bag, fully clothed, too warm to get inside. The campfire burned down. The camp lanterns were extinguished, until at last the circle was quiet. Gabe had left to check the perimeters, "Indians," he'd quipped when Jessie had asked what he thought he'd find.

Logically, she knew that the gold was under surveillance, but after the note of warning, she was uncomfortable. Finally, she crawled out from under the wagon. It was Gabe, she decided. His absence bothered her. As far as the world was concerned, the gold was safely locked in the box that was attached to the wagon. She had the only key. But something felt wrong.

She made a quick check of the campsite, then cut through the trees toward the river. Maybe she'd take a quick dip in the water, wash away some of the dust, and ease the tension that was keeping her mind spinning.

She wasn't the only one with that idea. The river water was being ruffled as someone swam across to the other side. She ducked behind a tree and watched as Gabe's golden hair caught the glimmer of moonlight before he reached the opposite shore and climbed out.

She watched, spellbound. He was always such a shock to her system, now more than usual. He stood and waded from waist-high water to the bank, wearing only his briefs.

What was he doing swimming across the river?

He disappeared into the trees, and she lost sight of him. Waiting in the darkness, unbidden thoughts raced through her. Everything from seeking privacy for personal needs to a rendezvous with person or persons unknown. The man assigned to ensure the safety of the gold could well be arranging its disappearance. Otherwise, why leave the camp side of the river?

Jessie waited. Long silent minutes passed. Finally, she decided there was only one way to know—cross the river and see for herself. Moments later, wearing only her bra and panties, she was submerged in the ice-cold water and swimming across the river. She'd always been a good swimmer, but she was tired from lack of sleep, and the water was very cold, too cold and too swift. She was being carried away from the camp. Suddenly, a cramp racked her leg, drawing it into a painful knot, and she went under.

Desperately, she struggled back to the surface. "Help!"

There was a splash. Then she felt a hand beneath her chin, a strong hand, pulling her toward the shore. "Relax, Jess. I've got you."

It was Gabe. "You're about to drown me!" she sputtered, trying to get away.

"You're the one taking the shortcut to town," Gabe said, lifting her and carrying her back to the bank where she'd left her clothes. He dropped to one knee and laid her on the ground. "What did you think you were doing out here?"

"I might ask you the same question."

"I needed to work off some tension."

She couldn't see his face in the darkness, but she felt the droplets of water fall from his hair onto her face and chest. Suddenly, she didn't feel cold. Suddenly, she realized that it was happening again—this electric connection that seemed to sizzle between them.

"I don't believe you," she snapped. "You met someone on the other side, didn't you?"

"Of course not. You didn't see anybody, did you?"

She had to answer truthfully, "No. But there was somebody there. Who was it, Gabe?"

"Ah, Jess. Believe me, I would never do anything to hurt you. I give you my word."

She lay beneath him, hardly daring to breathe, aware that while he'd tried to reassure her, he hadn't answered the question she'd asked.

He heard the sound of a car engine. In another moment Jessie would know she'd been right about his meeting someone. He had to do something to distract her.

He kissed her. And all the frustration of the last two days disappeared. Finally, when he pulled away, he gentled his voice. "I've missed you, Jess. Don't go away from me again."

She gasped and twisted away. "No. Let me go, Gabe. I'm cold."

"No you're not, Jessie. You're hot."

"Not anymore, Gabe," she said, and rolled away, coming to her feet. She pulled her shirt on, picked up her shoes and jeans, and dashed back through the woods to camp.

This time Jessie slid into her sleeping bag and pulled it up to her waist. She was shaking badly.

She was, as her song had said, quietly going crazy.

"Did you get it, Lonnie?" Gabe was kneeling down behind the Shorts' tent, whispering through the unzipped window.

"Certainly. And nobody saw us. Jane had Horace create a small diversion to cover our burglary."

"Pass the key to the lockbox under the edge of the tent, Lonnie, and hide the pouch until I ask for it."

"Are you certain we did the right thing, Gabe?" Jane asked. "I don't feel comfortable stealing from Jessie. I'm afraid she'll never forgive me."

"Believe me, Jane, this is the only way I can be sure that the gold is safe. Nobody will suspect the two of you."

Gabe told them good night and returned to the wagon from another direction. He, too, hated to deceive Jessie, but with any luck she wouldn't discover the pouch Jane had substituted contained rocks instead of gold nuggets.

Jessie didn't speak when he crawled into his sleeping bag. He could hear her breathing. He could almost feel her, she was so close, but she made no attempt to invite him closer. Now, no matter how much he wanted to share her bag, his guilty conscience wouldn't allow him to try.

Dammit all, he'd done what was necessary to protect Jessie, to make sure her gold got where it was supposed to be. Why did he feel like such a heel?

Because sooner or later they were going to make love, and then he would have done exactly what she'd accused him of—making love to her in return for something he wanted. This time he'd just done the taking first.

He lay there, wanting Jessie and feeling the guilt swell inside him. The sky overhead was filled with stars. Out here, away from the lights of the city, they were as bright as gold nuggets in a stream bed. Gathered around the edge of the campsite near the river were tall, stately pines that rustled in the night air, whispering as if they had witnessed the theft of the gold and were gossiping about it. In the center of the big circle the campfire crackled, glowing in the dark like a winking eye.

Everything seemed to be watching Gabe, even nature.

Above all, he was too conscious of Jessie there beside him, of her being so close that he could reach out and touch her if he wanted. And God knew, he wanted. He turned his head slightly, catching the scent of her, listening to the sound of her even breathing. Was it possible that she wasn't as affected by his presence as he was by hers? He thought that she was, or she was too silent. She was listening, feeling, feigning the deep, even breathing of sleep.

The weather forecast predicted the possibility of rain the next day. Fifty/fifty they said. He hoped the wet 50 percent didn't find them.

It was very late when Gabe finally went to sleep. And it seemed like only moments later that he was awakened by the sound of the camp rising. He opened his eyes. They felt as if he'd sprinkled them with river gravel. Staying awake for long periods of time was part of his normal job, but the kind of wakefulness he'd suffered for the last two nights was different.

And it didn't involve sleeping on the hard ground either, at least not since he'd been shot. His body complained as he shimmied out from under the wagon. There were the expected clouds in the sky, fulfilling the forecast for rain. He didn't look forward to that.

The wagon carrying the gold had a canvas cover, more authentic but less than satisfactory under the best of conditions. And Jane and Lonnie were sharing it. Only one other wagon had a cover, and it was a small farm wagon. If it did rain, Gabe could ride alongside. His Stetson was waterproof, and as part of his authentic costume, somebody at the sheriff's office had come up with a cowboy's split-tailed duster left over from some fundraising rodeo. The duster would cover everything but his feet.

But Jessie would be drenched. And knowing Jessie, she wouldn't get in the wagon. Gabe gave a worried look at the sky and hoped the rain held off until they got to the next campsite on Lake Lanier. At least there were indoor sleeping facilities nearby.

"I'm starved," Jane was saying as she crawled out of the tent. "Sleeping works up a powerful hunger."

Lonnie nodded. "Yes, we're having flapjacks, sorghum syrup, and fried fatback, just like my mother used to cook."

"Your mother was a gourmet cook, Lonnie Short, and the closest you've ever come to a fatback was on the dance floor of the Gold Dust Saloon. Morning, Gabe."

Gabe couldn't hide his smile. The couple's reparté was a refreshing relief from the heavy tension of uncertainty. He'd never known that kind of affection. Even his own mother hadn't cared about him. His father would never talk about her, and Uncle Buck had just said, "Good riddance," when she'd left. Several years ago Gabe had found her. She'd remarried, and she hadn't even seemed glad to see him.

Gabe glanced around. No sign of Jessie. Her bedroll was gone. That surprised him. He wouldn't have thought that she'd be able to get up and out without his hearing her. Maybe his senses were being dulled by lack of sleep. Or maybe it was simply sensual overload.

He scrubbed his chin, felt the stubble, and wished for a shower and his razor. He didn't know how real pioneers managed without scraping their skin away. He'd probably just let it go. A beard was more authentic-looking anyway, if he didn't itch to death in the meantime.

It was during breakfast that the couple driving the farm wagon confessed that the husband was suffering from a digestive upset and needed to go home. Lonnie and Jane transferred to the smaller wagon, and Gabe tied Blaze and Jessie's horse to the back of the Conestoga and took over the lead wagon, with Jessie on the seat beside him.

A constant stream of motorists who knew about the wagon train pulled off to watch them pass. Jessie was forced to smile and wave. The humidity increased, the clouds darkened, and the tension grew. Gabe searched for a safe topic of conversation, anything to chase away the growing tension. Then he remembered something that had bothered him.

"What did you mean on Sunday when you told Walter's wife that you'd get back to her?"

"I plan to make an offer for the farm. Walter doesn't want it. He's considering a new job in Tennessee."

"Why would you want it, Jessie? You said yourself that it wasn't a happy place anymore."

"Because it's my home. Even though I don't live there, it's the place . . . where I belong."

"I guess I don't understand that kind of attachment to a place. I never did. Places can become prisons."

"It isn't just a place, Gabe. It's all I have left of my family. It's where someone loved me, and I miss that."

Where someone loved me. Gabe didn't know how to answer that. He'd never found such a place on the mountain. Neither had the other St. Clair men, apparently.

"You know," he finally said, "giving Walter the money for the down payment was my last contact with my family. That's why he kept Blaze all these years."

"No, I didn't know."

"Uncle Buck will be the only one left up there, and the tourists who'll move in when he dies," Gabe observed.

Jessie fanned herself with the paper fan she'd found in her bag of authentic supplies behind the seat. "I always thought," she said quietly, "that mountain people were different from those elsewhere. Your neighbor was your neighbor, and he cared about you. But the new people moving to North Georgia aren't that way."

"The mountain people I knew were ornery and prejudiced."

"Pop James believed that we were special people; that no matter what the world might think about us, we were obligated to look after those we loved."

"And you bought that?" Gabe's voice was sharper than he'd intended. That was the same lie he'd been sold. "When did you find out different?"

"I guess when I waited for you to come back to me, and you didn't come. Have you seen Laura since you broke up?"

"Laura?" He repeated the name woodenly. For one long minute he couldn't even think who Laura was. All he could focus on was that Jessie had waited for him to come back, and he hadn't. "She called once, when I was home for my father's funeral, but I didn't see her."

"She married the banker. They have three children, but she seems a little lost. Funny, now that it doesn't matter anymore, we've become friends."

"Jessie, why didn't you leave after you graduated from college? You don't belong up there. You're smart. You've got an education. You've got ambition."

"I couldn't. It has something to do with being connected. Since I'm the only James left, I needed somewhere, or something, to belong to. I guess I don't have an answer that will make sense to you."

But she did, Gabe decided, and she'd already given it. She'd waited for him to come back to her. And he hadn't. Her aunts had died, then her grandfather, and finally her father. The mountain was the only family she had left.

For the next hour they rode, side by side, touching, reliving memories that were dangerous to both.

Gabe, constantly aware of the woman in the bright yellow shirt and blue jeans, felt his insides continue to tighten, as if he were being caught in a magnetic field that captured and held. He didn't want to know he might have been wrong in judging his family. His new life was fulfilling. He'd done well with the bureau, working his way up from a trainee to a special agent assigned to the federal men, volunteering for every job that took him away from the state.

But he still carried Pumpkinvine Mountain around with him, and he was beginning to suspect that meant Jessie James too.

Jessie finally broke the silence. "Your family could never understand why I've held on to that strip of land along the creek when it's too hilly for farming or building. Pop searched every inch of it for gold and didn't find any. But suppose he was right?"

"I suppose there could be more gold. There are still a few mines in North Georgia, aren't there?" Gabe asked.

"Sure, but for the most part they're small-time operations. Pop believed there was a vein that ran along the fault line from North Carolina down into Alabama. Somebody in Alabama is actually working a productive gold mine, and one day, who knows, I may still find that elusive vein if I can keep it out of your uncle's hands. Unless I need the money desperately, I'll never sell."

"Sooner or later they'll cut a road from the back, and Uncle Buck will buy another way in."

"How'd that ever happen anyway?" Jessie asked. "People always leave themselves a way to get to their land, even if the county doesn't force them."

"I don't know. It belonged to my grandmother. When my grandfather came back from the prison camp, she sold all the surrounding land. I guess she needed the money. This was before the famous poker game when old Evan won your grandfather's gold mine."

They were doing it again, Gabe decided, exchanging private confidences, talking about things that neither of them ever mentioned to anyone else. It had always been that way, their friendship, their openness. When had it all changed? When had they lost each other?

When he'd slept with her and she'd sent him away.

"Damn!" he swore, and gave old Horace a flick of the reins. To which Horace stopped, cocked one big brown eye back at the driver, and deposited what could be called fertilizer in the middle of a concrete road.

The rain held off. They reached Lake Lanier. In anticipation of the impending weather, the forward scouts had built a fire and had dinner waiting. Once again, the animals were fed and bedded down for the night. Nobody suggested that Jessie sing, for which she was grateful.

Later, as she unrolled the bedding, she was sorry they hadn't had a sing-along. At least that would have filled part of the time that loomed ahead. Here and there lanterns and portable radios came out of hiding, and the peacefulness of the trail disappeared as the announcers for the Atlanta Braves called the game. The team was already assured of a spot in the play-offs, but they had their minds on winning it all.

Last night had been cool. Tonight the air was humid, making the animals nervous and Jessie short-tempered. One more day and night and they would be at the capital. She'd have to change into her gingham dress and bonnet for the entry into the city.

Jessie decided against going down to the lake for a bath. She was afraid she might not get through the brush without running into a wild animal, without meeting Gabe.

Nothing came easy anymore.

The feud between the St. Clairs and the Jameses was as intense as ever. Except now it was personal.

SIX

They were halfway from Lake Lanier to Stone Mountain when they lost another wagon to a broken axle.

By the time they stopped for lunch, the train was behind schedule, and the sky was even more threatening. Jessie climbed down from the wagon, stretching her complaining muscles. She wasn't prepared for the sophisticated woman who met them holding a microphone in her hand.

"Miss James?" The woman, followed by a man with a camera, didn't wait for confirmation. "I'm Emily Moran, reporter with WXNA, Channel Fourteen. We've had a report that someone has threatened to hold up the wagon train."

"How'd you find out?" Gabe came to stand beside Jessie.

"We got a tip. Say, don't I know you?" the

reporter asked as she took a long look at Gabe. "Didn't I see you in that GBI—"

Gabe caught the reporter's arm and leaned down, giving her a quick kiss of greeting. "Hello, Miss Moran, nice to see you again."

But Gabe's quick move didn't completely conceal the curious look that passed over the reporter's face as he turned her away and walked her toward the mules.

Jessie was stunned. Who could have tipped off the media? The Sheriff's Department had promised to keep the threat quiet. And what were Gabe and the reporter whispering about? Jessie didn't miss the pleased nod of agreement given by the reporter as she allowed Gabe to lead her back to where Jessie was standing.

Jessie told herself to be polite. To be rude wouldn't foster the image of her grandfather's generosity, which, for Jessie, was the purpose of this trek. After giving Gabe a frown that told him exactly what she thought of his enthusiastic greeting for the reporter, Jessie planted a stiff smile on her face.

"I don't have much time. What can I do for you, Miss Moran?"

"I'd like to get a few shots of the wagon train and ask you some questions."

"Fine, come along. Let's find a place to sit." Jessie walked toward the chuck wagon and glanced around. There would be no campfire at lunch. The cook was handing out sandwiches and packages of chips. Jessie grabbed two cans of soft drinks and headed for a fallen log at the edge of the woods.

"Have a seat," she directed, giving the reporter's silk dress an amused look. Jessie offered her a soft drink.

Emily declined the offer and took a reluctant seat on the log. "I'd really prefer a shot of you with the wagon."

"But Horace would rather not be disturbed."

Emily looked confused. "Who's Horace?"

"He's our lead mule," Jessie said, taking a lesson from Jane, who always said the best method of handling adversity was to confuse the hell out of it. "He's impatient to get to Atlanta. He has a date waiting."

Emily frowned. "I don't understand."

"It's like this," Jane said, arriving as if she'd been sent for, "Horace's love life is confidential. We promised him secrecy. The real story here is Jessie. You know her grandfather originally mined this gold."

"Yes. That's very interesting, but what I really want to know about is the feud."

"What feud?" Jessie snapped, forgetting her plan to confuse and conquer.

"Between the St. Clairs and the Jameses. Did

Mr. James really lose his gold mine to Mr. St. Clair in a poker game?"

"Oh, yes," Jane said, answering for Jessie. "Just like the Hatfields and the McCoys, they were always feuding. But that poker game was a long time ago. Beware of repeating gossip about feuds and thieves."

"You mean the feud is over?"

"Absolutely," Gabe said, sitting down by Jessie. "I'm a St. Clair, and Jessie is the last of the James gang. We've settled our differences and teamed up to get the wagon train through."

But the reporter didn't give up. With the camera rolling she asked, "What about the threat of a holdup? Any sign of the outlaws yet?"

"No," Jane confided with an air of secrecy. "But if your viewers want to know the end of the story of the Jameses and the St. Clairs, they need to come to Gold Rush Days in Dahlonega next week. I'd recommend the Nugget Hotel and the Gold Dust Saloon. Did you know that Jessie is the singer with the Dusters?"

Jessie looked at Jane helplessly. She might have forgotten her plan to confuse and conquer, but Jane hadn't. Here she was on television doing a commercial for the festival, the hotel, and the saloon. The only thing she'd left out was the Museum and the clogging contest. Jessie decided she'd better get her out of there before she started selling tickets.

"I'm sorry, Miss Moran," Jessie said. "Take your pictures. If you need anything else, ask Gabe. He seems to have all the answers. Please excuse me."

Moments later the heavens opened, releasing a torrential downpour that had the reporter running for her van.

Jane headed for her wagon. Jessie was hunched inside the Conestoga, listening to the rain settle down to a light but steady downpour as it hit the wagon's canvas cover. Jessie checked the security box once more, shining a flashlight on the pouch. The pouch was still there—but the thread was gone.

Who? When? It didn't make sense. At least the intruder hadn't opened the bank pouch, setting off the red dye bomb she and the banker had secretly rigged up. The bag of gold was safe. Jessie tucked the threatening note inside and relocked the box just as Gabe climbed onto the wagon seat and drove the wagon down the road in the rain.

"What are you doing, Gabe?"

"Driving this wagon. A wagon train doesn't stop when the rain comes. We have to get to Stone Mountain Park tonight."

Jessie plundered through her bag, pulling out a fresh pair of jeans and a dry shirt.

"Don't look back," she directed.

"Why, will I turn into a pillar of salt?"

"Worse," she threatened. "I'll personally pulverize you, which you probably deserve anyway."

"Good, you're mad. At least you're talking to me. I thought we'd agreed to observe a truce for the duration of the journey."

"I lied," she said, pulling the shirt over her head. Had Gabe been the one to open the box? How? Of course a criminal would probably have ways. "What was Miss Moran talking about? A GBI what?"

"You must have misunderstood, Jessie," he began, then swallowed the words. What difference did it make if she knew what his real job was? Jessie wasn't the thief.

"Never mind," she said. "Even if you are an ex-con, I don't want to hear your excuse. It probably would be a lie anyway."

"I'm no ex-con," he swore. "And I'll tell you everything. I just have to do one thing first."

"What? Steal my gold? Or make love to me again?"

Gabe gave an exasperated sound. "I don't want your gold. I never wanted your gold, your land, or your . . ."

"Body? Is that what you're trying to find a delicate way to say?"

"I was thinking more about your heart."

"Forget that! I'm particular about who I fall in love with." Jessie climbed out of the back of the wagon, dragging a tarp as she took her seat beside him.

"I might as well. You never give me a chance to explain. I think you want me to be in the wrong. That makes it all right for you to be a martyr. What in hell are you doing out here in the rain anyway?"

"I'm playing the part. A pioneer woman wouldn't hide in the back of the wagon because it started to rain. She'd ride beside her man. And I'm no martyr."

Everything they said set off sparks, but Gabe felt himself smiling as he reached out, drawing the end of the tarp around his shoulders and capturing Jessie inside.

"Is that what I am," he said in her ear, "your man?"

This time it was Jessie who swore. "You heard me say that I'm playing the part. The emphasis is on acting, pretending, playing. Get yourself an umbrella."

Jessie jerked the tarp away and made a great show of covering her legs and feet. It wasn't working. She was already half-soaked again. She felt a great empathy for the pioneer women. At least Jessie knew she'd be home the next night, sleeping in her own bed above the Gold Dust Saloon.

"I liked it better when we shared the tarp," Gabe said.

"I'll bet you did!"

"What's really wrong, Jess? Why does being close to me make you so angry? A lot of people who care about each other sleep together."

"Not a James and a St. Clair."

"There you go tying our relationship to some ongoing feud between our families. Why not forget the past, do something for you, concentrate on your music?"

"You don't understand," she said, "nobody ever understands. Music is a pie-in-the-sky dream."

"You mean like finding gold?"

"Maybe, but that mountain is my road from the past to the future. Once it's gone, I won't belong anywhere."

"I'm sorry, Jess. I guess I don't understand. I think a person makes his own road."

Jessie felt the rain running down her collar. Angry motorists passed the wagons, blowing their horns and calling out ugly warnings as they were forced to battle, not only the elements, but the slow pace of the mules and horses.

"You might not feel that way if you were alone," she said.

"I am alone. I've chosen to be for almost ten years."

"And what kind of life do you live, Gabe?"

"I have a job I like, a small apartment, friends."

"Close friends, like we were?"

"No, I guess not. That kind of friendship doesn't come along every day."

She wanted to say, "You know that, and you walked away from it?" Instead she asked, "And that's enough?"

"I thought so. Now, I don't know, Jess."

"Have you ever been in love, Gabe?"

"No, I don't think so." How could he be? He'd made very sure he didn't get close enough to anybody to let it happen. "Other things have been more important," he said roughly.

"I don't think you're what you appear to be. Are you a thief?"

"Oh, Jessie. I'm not trying to steal your gold."

"That's good, for if you do, you'll be in for a big surprise."

If he wasn't lying, somebody was. He might not have stolen her gold yet, but he was up to something.

What was nagging at her conscience was that she was the biggest liar of all. She was the only one who knew that the pouch was empty.

The James Gang had already robbed the train.

Jessie sighed. They were back to the gold again. It had become the focus of both their frustrations and the mask behind which they retreated when open emotions threatened their newly emerging relationship.

As they rode, under the guise of scratching

his day-old growth of whiskers, Gabe covertly watched the change of expression on her face, an expression that grew ever more depressed. What would happen when she learned the truth, that she was the only suspect? Ben had sent word that there were no fingerprints on Joey's warning note. But it had been written on the back of a flyer advertising free drinks at the Gold Dust Saloon.

He didn't think Jessie would understand what he'd done. As far as she knew, she had the only key. The gold was still in the box. Or was it?

Jane and Lonnie had taken the pouch, but he was beginning to wonder if he shouldn't have checked the contents. Suppose he'd been the one who'd been hoodwinked?

Tonight, after they'd made camp, he'd open the bag. Once he'd verified its contents, he'd confess what he'd done to Jessie. She'd made it plain that she didn't want to relive the past, but the last thing he wanted to do this time when he left was have her believe that he'd used her.

He'd been toying with the idea of suggesting to Jessie that she consider coming to Atlanta for a visit, just in the interest of getting to know each other on neutral turf. That wouldn't interfere with her compulsion to buy back the James land. In fact, he'd even do what he could to help her.

The rain picked up again. To complicate matters, the wind turned even more brisk. Their arrival at the park would not be the triumphant entry Jane had prophesied or Jessie had envisioned.

When they finally spotted the entrance, it was already dark, the clouds and the rain closing out any view of the great mountain of rock. The laser show planned to announce their arrival had obviously been canceled. The park was empty of people.

The security guard explained that their campsite was set up under the trees around the lake. Jessie, miserable, cold, and hungry, quickly began to help Gabe feed the animals and settle them down for the night. At least they'd be protected somewhat by the tall, thick pine trees interspersed with hickory and maple trees.

Jessie tried very hard not to look at Gabe. She was tired, and her emotions were drawn into a thin thread of regret. Their journey was almost over. She needed to put some distance between them.

"I'll leave it to you to secure the animals and the campsite," she said as he stopped the team. "I'll check on Jane and Lonnie and see about our food for tonight."

"Fine," Gabe snapped. "I'll meet you back here as soon as I can."

They moved off in different directions, Jessie toward the spot where Lonnie and Jane were setting up their tent. She took hold of the mass of nylon and helped fit it over the aluminum skeleton that held it up while Jane pulled the tie-downs tight and fastened them to the stakes.

"You may be pretty uncomfortable on the ground tonight," Jessie said to Jane, giving her a long, searching look. "Are you sure you don't want to get your suitcase and check into the park hotel?"

Jane noticed the sharpness of Jessie's voice and winced. "No, we'll be fine."

"Gabe might need us," Lonnie added, refusing to look at Jessie. "You get along and make your own camp. You're soaked."

Jessie let out a deep sigh. "Soaked" was putting it mildly. She'd finally left the tarp on the wagon seat and let the rain finish the job it was intent on: death by drowning, or exposure.

With a growing sense of frustration Jessie turned away, heading for the mess wagon, where the cook was handing out thermoses of hot coffee and containers of chili and crackers. She claimed enough for her and Gabe and started back to the wagon.

The ground was saturated, leaving the water puddling where it couldn't find a place to run. Keeping dry was going to be a problem for everyone. From what she could see, the prediction that the participants might slip away to the park hotel was proving to be true. Jessie couldn't blame them. She felt sorry for the sheriff's men, forced to keep watch in such miserable conditions. She wished she'd never agreed to make the trip. They could have sent the gold into Atlanta in the sheriff's car.

Tomorrow it would be over. She'd simply have to be careful, keep her eyes on the gold pouch, and wait for the thief to make his, or her, move. Lordy, she was tired, and wet, and hungry. She put the coffee and food on the wagon seat and pulled herself up. She didn't know when Gabe would get back, and she didn't know what they'd do when he came.

Inside the wagon she pushed the supplies around, arranging space for her sleeping bag. She'd already decided to sleep in the wagon, even before the rain. She laid out the food and coffee on top of the lockbox containing the gold, along with a lantern that she'd found in one of the storage boxes. Lighting the wick made her feel better, for it cast a warm glow across the enclosure. The food could wait until she'd gotten out of her wet clothes.

From her backpack she pulled the last dry clean shirt she had, an oversized T-shirt that she often used to sleep in. Ripping the wet garments off, she pulled the soft cotton shirt over her bare body and replaced her sneakers with a pair of dry kneesocks.

Using the one towel she'd brought, she began

to dry her hair. The slow rhythm of the rain on the canvas cover was a lonely sound. She might be the only one on the wagon train, and she'd never know it. She'd been alone for most of her life, but here it was so complete.

Gradually, she worked herself around to the real problem. The trip was coming to an end. Gabe would be gone. She'd never dared hope that she would get a change to rekindle what they'd once shared. And she'd done everything wrong when she had the chance. She should have told him that she regretted her actions when she'd run away from him ten years before.

He loved her too. She knew he did. The feelings were still there, as strong as ever. They'd learned to hide them. The old Gabe wouldn't have been able to close them off so completely. But once he'd gotten off the mountain, he'd learned how to distance himself.

Outsiders wouldn't understand the fierce loyalty demanded of family members, even by those who didn't deserve it. For Jessie, it was a choice she made freely. But Gabe was smothered by his family.

She'd learned, bit by bit, about his uncle. Instead of being proud of Gabe's success, Buck put him down for it. "He has no business trying to be something he isn't," Buck had said. He'd even tried to use Gabe. Jessie wondered how he'd felt when Gabe hadn't fulfilled his mission to force her to grant the easement?

Until she'd talked to Walter's wife, Rachel, Jessie hadn't thought Gabe had any communication with his family, except to attend his father's funeral. Perhaps she'd been wrong. Maybe she was the only one he hadn't kept in touch with.

Now, he was leaving again, and she'd have to figure out how to get her life back to normal. All she had to do was get through the night.

After he saw to the animals, Gabe spoke by radio to his contact, arranging to meet him after midnight to transfer the gold. He also sent word to Ben that he intended to tell Jessie that he was an agent for the Georgia Bureau of Investigation. Maybe if she knew that he was a legitimate officer of the law, she'd quit worrying about him being the thief. What he'd done had been for the best, and he was sure she'd understand.

As he caught sight of the wagon, the hairs on the back of his neck suddenly stood straight up. All the tension he'd felt swirling around them for most of the trip suddenly concentrated in his abdomen, twisting his innards and pouring heat into every vessel.

Jessie was a silhouette, clearly revealed by the lantern inside the wagon. He watched, his heart thudding in his chest, as she unfastened her shirt and wiggled out of it, unzipped, and peeled her jeans down her legs, and shoved her wet clothes through the slit in the canvas to the seat outside. She patted herself dry, then raised her arms and slid some kind of garment over her body.

He began to move as she dropped to her feet. Before he realized what he was doing, he was climbing into the wagon. As it lurched beneath his weight, he heard a cry of alarm. When he pulled back the canvas, Jessie was pressed against the side of the lockbox, eyes filled with alarm, holding a thermos as if it were a lethal weapon and she were a javelin thrower in Olympic competition.

"What are you doing, Gabe?"

"I'm—I'm—" What in hell was he doing, scaring the life out of her? "Sorry, Jess. I didn't mean to frighten you. I guess I just lost it there for a minute."

"Lost it? What does that mean?"

She was still holding the thermos, but she was losing that frightened-deer look.

"Well, I saw you, I mean your silhouette, against the canvas, and I—"

"Oh. You watched me undress?" How could she have been so foolish? She'd seen enough movie scenes to know what light behind a screen could do. Why hadn't she thought?

"Sorry, I shouldn't have, but it caught me by surprise. I mean, it's as if we're the only two people left in the world, except for Jane and Lonnie, and they're only interested in each other."

"But we're not, are we, Gabe? We're just two people who keep bouncing into each other, like two of those little kissing figurines. If everything is just right, their magnets draw them together; otherwise, they fly apart like sparks from two live wires touching. Well, I'm tired of wanting you, Gabe. Go away."

"What's wrong, Jess? Talk to me. We've always been able to talk, no matter how deep we were stuck in the mud. What's going on here?"

"Gabe, believe me, I don't know what's going on. I don't know why you're here or why anybody would write threatening notes to me. And I don't know what you want from me, but I can't take it anymore."

"You've had a warning note. Where is it?"

"Just one, and I—I destroyed it."

"Jessie, I'm sorry. I should have leveled with you. And I will, but for now you'll have to trust me."

Jessie lowered the thermos and sat, eyes moist and lips trembling. "I think it's too late. You came back to protect the gold. There's nothing for you to worry about. The gold is safe. Go away, Gabe."

"Surely," Gabe said in a pained voice, "you aren't going to throw me out into the storm."

Jessie blanched. As if even the elements were conspiring against her, the rain increased its volume, drops hitting the canvas like a barrage of bullets. Inside the wagon, inside the circle of warm candlelight, it was almost cozy.

"No, I guess even I can't do that. I brought your supper, unless I've turned it into espresso." She lowered the thermos and held it out. "Sit down."

"I don't suppose you'd let me get out of these wet clothes first, would you?"

"Only if you put out the light."

He lifted his duffel bag, pulled out dry clothing, and blew out the lantern.

Jessie closed her eyes. It wasn't necessary; the darkness was complete. But even with her eyes closed, she could see Gabe. She didn't need her vision to see; she'd carried a picture of Gabe for most of her life.

"Do you remember the first time we ever went swimming without our clothes, Jess?"

"No!"

But she did. It had been that first summer. She'd been six, and he'd been ten when they'd played together at the lake. Neither had thought anything about seeing the other's body. Until the summer he was sixteen and his body had begun to do strange things. His voice had started to change, and a coating of light hair had feathered his chest, powerful even then.

Suddenly, Jessie had insisted that they wear swimming suits. Except she hadn't had a suit. She'd used a pair of shorts and a halter instead, and that's when their relationship had begun a subtle change. She still remembered the way she felt, the strange stirrings that had assaulted her twelve-year-old body, much like she was feeling now.

"No," she repeated, "but I remember the last time. I knew that you were the most handsome boy I'd ever seen and that it must be embarrassing for you to be seen with a kid like me."

Gabe gave a light laugh. "You thought it had something to do with you? Try being sixteen and having your hormones kick into gear when you least expect it, when you don't yet know how to deal with the physical evidence of those hormones."

"I always thought it was me," Jessie said softly.

"I didn't think so at the time, but now I look back and think you might be right. You were a kid, but you looked at me as if I were a man and made me feel like one as well."

"Was our entire relationship based on sex, Gabe?"

"Hell no. At least no more than most. Sex was the least of it, for me. I had nobody to talk to, to share my feelings with. The guys all tried to outbrag each other, and you never knew if they were telling the truth or trying to BS the rest of us. And sex was about all they talked about. With you, it was different. We talked about school, and life, and dreams."

And they had. Jessie remembered the long discussions about history, about the Greek myths and poetry. Gabe had joined the drama club, and she'd rehearsed with him, playing Juliet to his Romeo, Blanche to his Stanley.

That seemed so long ago, yet those times had shaped both their lives. Certainly, when she joined the drama club in college, she hadn't done it because of Gabe. Yet every song she sang was to him.

At least in her mind.

When she'd returned to Dahlonega, it had been to show the town and Gabe that the Jameses were respectable. She could have gone somewhere else, but that would have severed her ties with everything important in her life.

Her past. Gabe. But Gabe hadn't come home again, and becoming the success she'd envisioned hadn't quite worked out. Still, she'd stuck it out, and little by little she'd created a life without Gabe as the focal point.

Now, here in the darkness, memories came rushing back. Her heart was racing, and she was finding it hard to breathe.

She felt the floor of the wagon shift as Gabe's knees touched the side of her foot. This was what she'd been waiting for, yet now she was unsure. Gabe hadn't come back to her; he'd come back to do a job. "Don't do this, Gabe," she said in a hoarse voice. "Don't do it to me again."

"Ah, Jessie, I don't think we can stop it," he answered, and crept forward in the darkness. "I've missed you. It's as if I'm coming back to life. For so long I haven't allowed myself to do anything but work. The world is so crazy out there. Tonight I just want to forget, to hold you the way I used to before it all comes to an end."

Gabe was right. Tomorrow would bring an end to this lovely fantasy they'd been given. And that's what it was, a fantasy, a little girl's wish on a star. He'd leave, and it would all be over. The pain would come again. But she had Gabe, for now. And she did want him to hold her one last time.

"You can go home again," she whispered, and opened her arms, "at least for one night."

And then Gabe kissed her.

Jessie was barely breathing, her entire body caught up in a swirl of sensation. Familiar excitement, wonder, urgency, but above all, the sure knowledge that this was Gabe and he was loving her again.

"I like the nightshirt, Jess. It's soft and—and," he groaned, "you aren't wearing anything under it. Aren't you cold?"

"You're the one who's cold," she whispered, rubbing her hands over his bare chest, kissing him, drawing the heat that raged in his lower body upward.

"No, I'm warm, very warm."

Gabe slid down onto the bedroll, pulling her over him. He put his hands beneath her shirt, spreading his fingers across her breasts, parting his legs to allow her to fit between them. He loved touching her, feeling her hesitant movements as she responded to his touch.

It was at that point for Jessie that everything spun out of control. The light from the lantern seemed to reappear, shattered into a thousand little golden reflections behind her eyelids. The silky texture of his chest hair rubbing against her nipples, the feel of his lips brushing her neck and cheeks, all elicited a moan of pleasure.

But more than touch and taste, this was like coming home, like welcoming sunlight through the clouds, as if they were rolled up in a cottony cocoon that softened every movement into an exquisite kaleidoscope of sensation.

This time his invasion of her body was slow,

deliberately slow, drawn out as if he wanted to draw every semblance of tenderness from the moment. The feelings built into ever-quicker thrusts, deeper yet still restrained, as if both understood that when they let go, they would never be able to rein in their emotions again.

There was a wondrous feeling that encapsulated them, a whole new world not confined to place or time. Mountains, lakes, streams, the memories of all those things existed in the recesses of Jessie's mind, but it was Gabe who filled it and her body with himself. For this night he was her world, all that she'd ever wanted, all that she hoped to be.

Gabriel, an angel. Gabriel, her love.

SEVEN

Later, when they lay exhausted, sated with the taste and touch of each other, they covered themselves with the inner layer of the sleeping bag and lay silently in the darkness. Gabe pulled Jessie into the crook of his arm. "Where'd we go wrong, Jess?"

"I think it was the mountain. It was my protection and your prison."

"Why would that be?" He was trying to still the thundering aftermath of the desire that coursed through him. Every time he kissed Jessie, he was reminded that it was still there. He'd stopped fighting it. They had hours before the morning, before he had to go. This time loving Jessie had been different. She'd kissed him back because she wanted to, not because she didn't know what she was doing. And to his surprise he knew that was what he felt as well.

"I don't know, Gabe, why do you care? This will all be over tomorrow. This is our last night together." She gave a strained laugh. "That's the history of our relationship, isn't it? Each meeting is hello and good-bye."

Good-bye? That thought hit him in the gut. He didn't want the weekend to end. There were so many things about his life now that Gabe wanted to share with Jessie. He wanted to introduce her to his friends Gavin and Stacy Magadan, show her Underground Atlanta, take her to a concert at the Fox Theater.

He wanted to see and do all the things he'd done since college over again, sharing them with Jessie, seeing them through her eyes.

"Suppose it wasn't a last meeting, Jess? Suppose you moved to Atlanta. You could pursue your music. You could even operate a saloon there."

"Suppose you came back home, Gabe? We—you—could build a house on the lake. I could operate the saloon I already have, and you could—could run for mayor if you want to stay in politics."

That brought a laugh. "A St. Clair as mayor? Wow!"

Jessie burrowed her face against his chest. "Gabe, if there's something wrong in your past, we can fix it. I'll stand by you, no matter what."

She still believed that he was a criminal. And she was willing to stand by him. Gabe felt like a heel. He couldn't keep his promise anymore. "Jessie, about my past. I promised to tell you the truth."

"No! Not now. I don't want anything to spoil this night," she said, and closed off his protest with a kiss.

They ate the chili, drank the coffee, and made love again. There was no more talk about tomorrow, about either one moving to the other's place of residence. It was as if they'd silently accepted that this was another in a lifetime of good-byes.

They fell asleep in each other's arms. When he woke, the first rays of light were breaking the sky. He was late meeting his contact, almost six hours late. Reluctantly, he separated himself from her, pulled on dry clothes, and crept from the wagon, glad to discover that the rain had finally stopped. He hated to disturb Jane to take the bank pouch, but she assured him that she wasn't asleep. He could feel the smile on her face even if he couldn't see it.

"I'm glad you decided to move into the wagon," she said. "You certainly took your time."

He didn't answer. He wasn't feeling so good

about what he had to do. In fact, he felt like a double-crossing cheat. Jessie had accused him of making love to her every time he needed something, of using her feelings for him as some kind of bribe, and it was happening again.

But dammit, he was under assignment to protect the gold, and now he needed to protect Jessie's feelings as well. Whatever he found, he wasn't certain he'd be able to carry out his duty and satisfy his heart. Taking the money pouch, he made his way through the park to the antebellum mansion where he was to meet his contact.

Ben Jansen stepped from the shadows. "Joe decided there was something wrong and sent for me when you didn't show up on time. I was beginning to think you weren't coming."

"Ben, I didn't expect you."

"When I got word that you were about to blow your cover, I thought I'd check on you personally. What's the problem?"

"I don't know. I don't know that there is one. I just feel that something is wrong."

"Is that why you're carrying the pouch? I thought you had it hidden in a safe place until tomorrow—no, make that today."

"I did. But I think we need to open this pouch now, just to make sure the gold is safe."

"Fine, open it."

"Do you have a flashlight?"

"Right here." A circle of light was directed on the bank bag.

But it wasn't easy. Gabe looked at the pouch for a long time, turning it over and over in his hands. If he forced it open and the gold was still there, he'd feel like a fool for having questioned Jessie, but if it was empty, what then?

Ben held out his hand. "Want me to do it, Gabe?"

"No, it's my problem. I'll do it." He inserted his duplicate key into the lock on the pouch and slowly pulled it open.

The blast caught him by surprise. The shower of red powder that splattered his face and clothing astonished him. But not as much as the empty pouch he was holding. There was nothing inside. The sides of the bag had been weighted with soft lead so that the weight was right, but there was no way of determining the contents.

He'd opened an empty bag.

There was no gold.

And he was covered with red powder that pronounced his guilt without question. She'd played him for a fool.

"Now what?" Ben asked seriously.

It was the toughest question Gabe ever answered. Any solution he reached turned into good-bye. With a heavy heart he gave the only answer he could. "Now we go after the James Gang. Let's go raid a wagon train."

Followed by his superior officer, Gabe strode back through the woods, the wet limbs reaching out to shake their droplets of moisture over his face. By the time he stormed aboard the wagon and Jessie opened her eyes, he looked as if he'd encountered a monster in the woods.

"Gabe, what's wrong?"

Jessie sat up, caught sight of the second man holding the flashlight behind Gabe, and let out a scream. "Gabe, you're hurt! If it's the gold he wants, he can have it."

"You rigged the pouch. There is no gold, Jessie. Where is it?"

Incredulity washed across her face as she understood what she was seeing on his face and shirt. "You stole my pouch? You opened it?"

"Yes, I did, Jessie. And the only thing I found was a dye bomb."

She came to her knees, covering herself with the sleeping bag. "You took my gold? You're the thief?"

"Dammit, Jessie! I'm an agent for the GBI. I'm no thief! But somebody sure as hell is."

"Wait! Wait!" Jane and Lonnie Short scrambled from their tent and hurried over to the back of the wagon. "He didn't take it, Jessie, we did.

We didn't want anything to happen to the gold, Jessie. Don't blame Gabe."

"I thought you were my friend," Jessie said, still staring at the red dye running down Gabe's face.

"I am," Gabe began.

"I loved you. I've always loved you."

"Jess, I—"

"Get out, Gabe. I want to dress," she said, and waited for the voyeurs to leave.

Ben Jansen cut off the light and moved toward the elderly man and woman wearing matching shorty pajamas and standing beside the front of the wagon. "And you are?" he asked.

"Jane and Lonnie Short," Jane answered. "My sister, Alice, is a friend of the governor's."

"Ah, yes, Alice's sister. How'd you get involved in this?"

"Well, I was trying to figure a way to get Jessie and Gabe together. It all started with Alice's idea that Gabe should protect Jessie's gold."

Gabe heard Jane's prattle, but it didn't penetrate the disturbing emotions that swirled around inside him. He wanted to explain to Jessie, then realized that it was too late. The look in her eyes reflected disbelief at first, then the sure dawning of cold understanding.

Flushed cheeks and rapid breathing gave further credence to Jessie's escalating anger as she clutched the bedroll.

"Nothing ever changes, does it? I guess you can't go home again, Gabe, even for one weekend. I should have known."

"Where is the gold, Jessie?"

"The gold is safe, Gabe. It will be at the capitol tomorrow, just like my grandfather wanted. I don't need you or anybody else to get it there. I never did."

She opened the locked box, lifted the substitute pouch, and threw it out the opening in the canvas. Then, not waiting to see if Gabe was watching, she dropped the bedding and began to pull on underwear, the red calico dress, and the matching bonnet. Once dressed, she looked up and caught sight of Gabe still standing there.

"I want you out of this wagon and out of my life, Gabriel St. Clair. You're not golden anymore, and I don't need a dark angel hovering over me, now or ever."

"Gabe?" Ben called from outside the wagon. "Will you look at this?"

Gabe stepped over the seat and dropped to the ground. "What?"

Ben opened Jane and Lonnie's substitute pouch, and a scattering of rocks and brightly colored marbles of assorted sizes bounced to the ground.

"Marbles?" he questioned.

"Well, Jane didn't think the rocks were quite

right. They were all the same size. The marbles were her idea."

"So, Gabe," Ben asked patiently, "where is the gold?"

"I suppose Jessie's gone to get it," Jane said.

"What do you mean, gone?"

Gabe strode back to the wagon, jerking the canvas cover open. The wagon was empty.

"Dammit, she's gone."

"Where would she go?" Ben asked. "She'd have to know we're coming after her."

"Who knows?" Gabe answered, his mind searching wildly for answers. "All I can tell you is she's wearing a red calico pioneer dress and bonnet."

"Let's split up and look," Jane suggested.

"Lonnie, find the sheriff's men and tell them what happened," Gabe directed.

Gabe searched the wagon one last time, including the lockbox. In the bottom he saw a piece of paper. *He isn't what he seems. Beware!* Jessie's note. Puzzled, he stuck it in his pocket to show to Ben and rejoined the search. Something about those words sounded familiar.

Moments later they had covered the entire campsite. There was no sign of Jessie James. Both she and the gold were missing.

The search was expanded to cover the entire park, including the mountain. To no avail. Finally,

Jane put both hands on her hips and started giving orders.

"Now I don't know what has happened here," she said, "but I know Jessie, and the most important thing in her life, other than her mountain, was getting her grandfather's gold to the state capitol. I don't know what happened, but I intend to get this wagon train there on time. Lonnie, you drive Jessie's wagon, and I'll drive ours."

"Good idea, Jane," Lonnie agreed. "I'll hitch up the animals."

Gabe followed Lonnie to the area where they had secured the mules and wagon horses. Other members of the train followed. They'd come this far; they might as well go all the way.

The park was bright in the fall sunshine. The rain the night before had washed all the haze from the air, and the sun's rays reflected off the highest peak of the huge granite mountain like a halo. It was a beautiful day for a jailbreak.

"He's gone, Gabe," Lonnie said in amazement. "Horace is gone. They're all gone, the horses and the mules. She must have let them go. Why?"

Jane and Gabe looked at each other, realization dawning.

"She didn't just let them go," they both said at the same time, "she's stolen them."

"And," Gabe added, heading for four-wheel

drive that Ben had driven, "she's got an hour's head start. Let's go, Ben."

"We're right behind you, Gabe. We'll meet you at the capitol," Jane called out. "Hitch up one of the sheriff's cars to this wagon. We're going to drive this sucker to the governor's office one way or the other."

But the patrol car refused to start. None of the vehicles would run. Jessie had disabled every one of them.

Even Ben Jansen's Jeep coughed a few times and died. They'd been hoodwinked. Quickly, Ben called for assistance, but assistance took time, and Jessie was moving on.

Gabe and Ben made their way to the stone posts at the park entrance, encountering the security guard who opened the park at first light.

"Have you seen a woman riding a mule?" Gabe asked.

"Sure did, over an hour ago. She came through here like one of them generals on the mountain leading a charge."

"Where would she go, Gabe?" Ben asked.

"I don't know. Can you arrange to put out an all-points bulletin? Somebody has to have seen her."

"But it's Saturday, and this is Atlanta. Crazy things happen all the time. It's possible that nobody even noticed."

"I'll find her, Ben."

Ben used his short-wave radio to signal Joe at headquarters. "Joe, have the police put out a lookout for a dark-haired woman wearing a red calico dress." Then he added in a pained voice, "Riding a mule."

There was a sputter on the other end of the phone. "What was that? She's riding a mule?"

"That's what I said. Just let us know if she's spotted. I don't think we want to stop her."

"Shall I say she's armed and considered dangerous?"

Gabe let out a wry laugh.

"You can say that," Ben answered. "You can certainly say that."

"Does this fugitive have a name?" the officer asked curiously.

"This fugitive definitely has a name," Gabe snapped. "She's Jessie James."

When the car arrived, Gabe took the wheel and headed toward town. He didn't know what else to do. He'd never believe that Jessie was a thief. Like Jane, he was convinced that delivering the gold was important to Jessie, so it seemed logical that she'd find a way to follow through.

"Didn't you check the pouch before you loaded it?" Ben asked curiously.

"We watched Jessie open the safety-deposit box and remove the pouch. She handed it to the sheriff, who signed for it and moved it, under guard, to the lockbox in the wagon. It never left our sight."

"But it was Jessie's safety-deposit box," Ben commented, "and she did have a key."

Gabe shook his head. "Jessie wouldn't have—"

"Somebody did." Ben reached for the radio. "Joe, get in touch with the Bank of Dahlonega. Find out if Jessie visited the vault before the gold was removed."

"I don't think they'll be open yet, sir."

"Then wake them up. We're after Jessie James. Over and out," Ben said, releasing the "talk" button. "You okay, Gabe?"

"How the hell do I know? I'm a special agent with the GBI, and I can't protect a wagon train carrying one little pouch of gold nuggets and dust." *I can't even protect the woman I love.*

"Ben, Joe here. There's been a report of a woman on a mule on the other side of Druid Hills. She rode through a woman's backyard, caught her clothesline, and ripped it from the pole. The woman's mad as a hornet—said the last time she saw her, the suspect was riding like a bat out of hell, with a granny gown caught on the mule's tail."

Gabe would have laughed if he hadn't been so worried.

Being worried didn't stop Ben. He chuckled as Gabe cut down East Ponce de Leon and headed for Druid Hills. It crossed his mind briefly that this was the general area where that movie company had filmed *Driving Miss Daisy*. There was the same kind of stubbornness in both Jessie and Miss Daisy. When Jessie James reached retirement age, she'd be just as cantankerous. He'd also bet that mule was traveling faster than Daisy's automobile.

Capturing this fugitive was proving very interesting. A state patrol car pulled in beside them, blue lights blinking. The driver gave a wave to Ben and whipped past, clearing the traffic away.

"Gabe, I'm not sure how safe it is for us to pursue Jessie. We might spook her and force her to do something stupid."

Gabe looked at his boss in disbelief. "Jessie do something stupid? You've got to be kidding."

Ben flicked on the radio again. "This is Captain Ben Jansen. Attention all units in pursuit of the woman on the mule. We do not want to apprehend. Turn off your lights, fall back, and follow at a safe distance."

Gabe cut back his speed to a slow crawl, listening as the police cars monitored her progress. "She's made it to Peachtree Street," Joe's voice said over the radio. "Looks like she's going downtown."

"Gabe, do you think she's heading for the capitol?"

"Why go all the way to Peachtree Street? She could cut down a side street and get to the capitol quicker. I don't understand."

The police car leading the procession had killed its blue lights and cut its speed to a crawl. Now, as Gabe reached the car, it pulled over and allowed the agents to pass. Then he saw her.

Jessie James, bonnet dangling by its ribbons and flying behind her, was riding Horace hell-for-leather down Peachtree Street. Early joggers watched in amazement. Drivers gave her a clear path. Pedestrians jumped back, allowing her to continue her mad dash.

Luck, or a higher angel, seemed to be with her. As she reached a traffic light, it miraculously turned green so that she never slowed her pace. In the middle of downtown Atlanta she suddenly turned right, forcing Gabe to plunge headlong into a one-way street. Car horns blared as Gabe maneuvered his vehicle around the traffic.

"Where in hell is she going?" Gabe said, swearing again as he lost sight of her behind a delivery truck.

Ben leaned out the window, trying to spot

her again. "My friend, it looks like she's about to abandon the mule."

Then Gabe spotted her, riding Horace into the Greyhound Bus Station.

"Damn," he swore. "She's going to hijack a bus!"

EIGHT

"Go back to Peachtree and head north," Jessie whispered in Horace's ear. "The vis-à-vis carriage stand is right there." She slapped him on the rear. "Go for it, boy!"

The mule galloped away. At the same time Jessie ran inside the bus station. Gabe whipped around the mule, parked the company car, and followed. Ben directed the officers to block off the station and went after Gabe.

Inside the station Jessie slowed her frantic dash to a sedate walk and made her way to the baggage-claim area. "Excuse me?"

The sallow-faced man behind the barred counter turned to face her. "Something I can do for you?"

"Yes. I shipped a package from Dahlonega to Atlanta. I'd like to pick it up, please."

The worker eyed Jessie's odd attire, her hair, dried by her wild ride into town, and the bonnet hanging down her back. "What's the name?"

"Jessie James."

"Sure, and I'm the Church Lady."

"No, really. You have a box, a wooden wine crate. It's addressed to Jessie James, to be held for pickup."

His expression said plain enough that he didn't believe her, but he finally turned to the rows of packages and cases behind him.

Gabe, watching from the doorway, took a step into the waiting room and stopped at the end of the row of seats. A disreputable man who was sleeping in the seat at the end opened one eye and let out a yell.

"Don't hurt me!"

Gabe looked around, unable to comprehend what had set off the man. Then he remembered Jessie's bomb and looked down at the rivers of red dried across his shirt.

"Sorry, sir," he said quietly. "I've just had a run-in with a can of red dye."

He dodged around the seat and headed toward Jessie, who was giving the bus employee behind the caged counter a piece of her mind.

"No, I don't have any identification. I didn't bring my purse. No, I didn't drive my car. As a matter of fact, I rode in on a mule."

"Now don't get smart with me, lady."

"I'm not getting smart," she yelled. "And my name is Jessie James. As a matter of fact," she said, lowering her voice threateningly, "I have a gun, and if you don't give me my package, I'm going to show you a new way to get a haircut."

She lifted the corner of her skirt and draped it over her hand, extending her finger in such a way that he would understand that the hidden object was a gun.

"You're holding me up?" the clerk asked incredulously.

"I'm trying," she snapped. "Now, give me that box, and I won't hurt you. Otherwise . . ."

"I don't think so, Jessie," Gabe said, appearing at her side. "I wouldn't want anybody else to be wounded."

The employee took one look at Gabe, slid the package across the counter, and slumped to the floor out of sight.

"Now look what you did, Jessie. You scared the poor man to death."

"He deserved it," she said, dropping her skirt and tugging the box through the opening.

"What's in the box, Jess?"

"Gold, Mr. GBI agent. The gold my grandfather mined and left to use on the capitol dome." She slid the box forward, grabbing it with both hands, and carried it out the door, straight into Ben Jansen.

"Let go of my box!"

"I don't think so, Miss James. I'm Ben Jansen, the chief of the Atlanta bureau of the GBI. Suppose we find some place private and open your box."

"Fine!" she said sharply. "Just as long as we get it to the capitol on time."

They put the box in the back of the car and drove over to the complex of government buildings, parking behind the golden-domed building in a private garage.

"We'll go up to the office," Ben said. "We can open the box, and Gabe can clean himself up a bit."

A subdued Jessie allowed herself to be directed to Gabe's office. She didn't resist, and she didn't comment. It seemed to Gabe that she wanted to get it over with.

Joe, who was still waiting, looked up, swallowed a startled grin, and watched the three walk into Gabe's office and close the door. Moments later, Ben exited the office and returned with a screwdriver.

Inside the room Ben pried the top from the case, revealing a dusty brown bag. He lifted it, shaking it gently before loosening the drawstrings and emptying the contents on the desk—rocks, iron ore, river pebbles made smooth by eons of Pumpkinvine Creek passing over them.

Gabe raised startled eyes to Jessie's.

"But I don't understand," she whispered.

"Where is the gold, Jessie?" Gabe asked.

"It's there. It has to be. Nobody has opened that bag since it was placed in the safety-deposit box. I swear it!"

"You didn't open it?" Ben asked.

"No. I put it in my purse, then in this box, then shipped it. I didn't believe all that business about being held up, but I didn't want to take a chance."

Gabe shook his head in disbelief. "So you shipped a sack of rocks to Atlanta on a Greyhound bus?" He began to laugh.

Silent tears rolled down Jessie's face.

Ben studied the pouch, ran his hand inside, and pulled something out. A rumpled sheet of paper. "Wait, the bag isn't empty."

"What?" Jessie watched him pull out a sheet of paper. She recognized her grandfather's spidery handwriting, and took the letter and began to read.

If you're looking at this, Jess, it will mean that there's no gold. I'm sorry. There never was any gold in here. I didn't want to tell anybody, for I thought the vein ran beneath the creek onto our property and I'd find it again. But I was wrong.

I guess you ought to know it all. The poker game was fixed.

"I knew it!" Jessie exclaimed. "I always knew it. Pop was the best player in North Georgia. Evan was a crook."

I made sure of it. It was my way of looking after Martha, the only way I could.

"Martha?" Ben questioned. "Who's Martha?"
"My grandmother," Gabe answered in a low voice.

We fell in love while Evan was off in the war. She was going to divorce him when he got back. Then he got captured and she couldn't. When he finally did get home he was all messed up and she couldn't leave him. He could never support her, and those sorry St. Clairs would have let Martha starve to death. It was the only way to see that she was taken care of properly.
Her husband certainly couldn't. I didn't know then that you'd come along all these years later.

Gabe let out a deep breath. All his life, until it played out, his family had lived on the proceeds from the mine, a mine that should have belonged to Jessie.

Jessie was equally stunned. All her life she'd hated the St. Clairs, except for Gabe, because they'd cheated her grandfather out of his mine. But Pop was the one who'd cheated, by loving another man's wife.

"Well, there's no thief," Ben observed. "I'd better tell the governor."

"No, wait," Gabe said. Jessie would never live down the shame if they announced her grandfather's fraud. "Just hand over the pouch, and don't say anything about its being empty. If it hadn't been for my family, there would be gold inside the pouch. I'll replace it, personally."

"Absolutely not!" Jessie snapped. "I'll issue a public apology and supply the gold myself."

"From where?" Gabe hated pinning Jessie down, but it was necessary. But she couldn't be allowed to either delude herself or do something that would ruin her for life.

"I'll sell the saloon," she said.

"You can't do that, Jessie," Gabe argued. "It's too important to you. There has to be another way. Besides, from what I understand about your finances, that won't be enough."

"Then I'll sell my piece of the mountain."

"No, I won't let you. I'll . . ." Gabe struggled for words, answers. For the last two days he had tried to figure out a way to get her off that mountain. Now that it had come, he couldn't take it. He did love Jessie, but loving somebody was honoring their needs, and Jessie had made plain her need for her land.

"Sell me that easement, Jessie. That way you'll get to keep your land."

She looked at him with horror on her face. "It's finally come, hasn't it? You found a way to get what you wanted."

He could see it in her eyes. All the old doubts came hurtling back. Every time she gave herself to him, he took her love and left. *You'll never believe it, but you're wrong, outlaw. I'm doing this because I love you.*

"Believe what you like" was all he could say.

"I guess I don't have a choice. I'll have the papers drawn up. What do we do about the ceremony, Mr. Jansen?"

"My men rounded up the other mules and horses. The wagon train is on schedule, more or less. If we hurry, we can intercept the wagon and make the presentation on time. It wouldn't be unusual for the presentation to be symbolic. That was the recommendation of our office in the beginning. You can make whatever arrangements you choose in plenty of time to begin the repair work."

"Fine," Gabe said, taking Jessie's arm, "let's go."

Ben started to repackage the bag. "Wait, there's something else in the pouch." Ben pulled out a yellowed newspaper clipping. He glanced at it and handed it to Jessie.

"What now?" Gabe looked over her shoulder, reading, " 'Local Resident Killed Crossing Peachtree.' Who is it?"

"My mother," Jessie said, the color draining from her face. "She didn't even live on the mountain. She was killed in Atlanta. Daddy never told me that. Why would he do that, Gabe?"

Gabe had no answers. He had enough trouble understanding a man who took his own life. "Maybe he knew how you felt about the mountain. He didn't want to destroy your peace of mind."

"You always say maybe, Gabe. I was always the one who was sure of everything. That's funny, isn't it? Turns out you were right to question."

"Ah, Gabe," Ben said, "about cleaning up. I don't think you want to go on television looking like you've survived a massacre."

Half an hour later Gabe, wearing a fresh shirt, and Jessie, her hair neatly combed and covered by her bonnet, drove the Conestoga wagon to the steps of the state capitol and, with the world watching, presented an empty pouch to the governor.

Miss Emily Moran was the first reporter to head for the couple after the ceremonies.

"Did you discover who the outlaw was, Miss James?" She was holding the microphone out to Jessie.

"There was no outlaw," Gabe said smoothly. "The tip was a hoax."

"Why would someone do such a thing?" she asked, turning the mike toward Gabe.

"It was just part of the fantasy," Jane Short said. "Beware, a thing isn't always what it seems. What better way to give publicity to the reenactment and to the Gold Rush Days Festival beginning next week?"

And before the reporter could direct another question, Jane had taken over the mike and was shamelessly giving the festival another free commercial plug.

"What about the tip?" Jessie asked Ben as she tried to move away from the crowd.

"You know," he observed, watching Jane's animated attempt to keep Emily from wrestling the microphone away. He pulled Jessie's note from his pocket and read it. "He isn't what he seems. Beware!"

"Where'd you get that?"

"Found it in the wagon. I assume it was sent to you."

"Yes. Someone slid it under my door."

"I'll bet if we did a voice analysis of the anonymous caller, we'd find that it was a woman."

"Jane?" Jessie should have been astounded, but somehow she wasn't. Ever since Jane and Lonnie had turned up in Dahlonega, Jane had found one way after another to bring in business to both the hotel and the saloon. It had been Jane who had arranged for the music producer to come and listen to the band. It was Jane who came up with giving western dance lessons, clogging, even a Wednesday evening talent show. And everybody who stayed in the hotel got free coupons for drinks at the bar.

"Jane," Gabe echoed. It was beginning to make some kind of sense. He'd always liked going to Gavin Magadan's home. And once he met Gavin's mother, Alice, he'd heard about the outrageous Jane who'd fallen in love with a diesel mechanic and married him. Nobody had been surprised when she and Lonnie had headed for North Georgia and bought a hotel. Jane always went where the wind blew.

They'd left the crowded steps behind. Jessie wanted desperately to get back to Dahlonega and away from Gabe.

"The one good thing to come out of this is that everybody in the state will know about Gold Rush Days. I guess I'd better get started, or there will be so much traffic, we'll never get the wagons back. Good-bye, Gabe, and thank you. I guess you are my guardian angel after all."

"Oh, no, you don't, Jessie James. This is one good-bye that isn't happening, at least not yet."

"I don't know what you mean, Gabe. I'm tired, and I'm ready to go home."

"You can't. The governor has invited us to dinner, and it would be rude to refuse."

"Nobody is invited to dine at the governor's mansion on the spur of the moment, Gabe."

"No? You don't know Governor Diller. He likes country music, and once he found out you were a singer, he insisted that we join him."

"But I don't have anything to wear, and I don't feel much like a party." Truthfully, the headache she'd headed off all morning was descending with the force of an anvil. She wanted a bath and clean clothes and food, in that order.

"Nobody turns down an invitation to the governor's mansion, Jessie. Aren't you afraid that it might make Emily Moran suspicious? You don't want that, do you?"

"You mean she might find out there was no gold? How?"

"Reporters are like smoke, they can get into locked rooms and pouches too."

"Well, I'm not going. I don't have anything to wear."

"It's only one o'clock in the afternoon, Jessie. The governor's dinner isn't until seven. Jane's already working on the problem. Between her and Alice, they'll come up with something. I'm to take you to the Magadan house."

Jessie reluctantly allowed herself to be led away. She was too tired to argue. Too much had happened. She'd found out her grandfather was a liar and a cheat, that he'd coveted another man's wife and purposely lost his gold mine in a poker game. She'd learned that her mother hadn't been killed in an accident in Lumpkin County because she'd never lived in Lumpkin County.

But more than that, she'd found out that Gabe had been assigned to keep her from stealing the gold that was never there in the first place because they thought she was the thief. He'd made love to her even when he hadn't trusted her.

But she'd let him make love to her when she hadn't trusted him.

And now, after all these years, he'd found a way to take away her part of her mountain, just as the St. Clairs always planned. She was so confused.

"All right, Gabe, let's go."

Gabe drove the company car down Peachtree to West Paces Ferry Road, turning off before they reached the governor's mansion.

Jessie leaned her head against the back of the seat and closed her eyes until he reached the Magadan home where Jane was waiting.

Gabe watched as Jessie, eyes glazed with resignation, her steps slow in defeat, followed Jane.

"Why did you do it, Pop James? Why did you let her go on thinking the gold was there?"

But there was no answer.

Gabe decided there never had been.

This time Jessie didn't even say good-bye.

"I hope you're not still angry with us, Jessie," Jane was saying as she led Jessie up the stairs. "But when Gabe explained what was happening, we couldn't refuse to help, not when it was my fault that wild story ever got started."

Jessie was certain that Jane held the answer to part of the confusion, but Jessie didn't want to hear it. In fact, she listened to very little of Jane's chatter. It didn't seem to matter whether she answered or not. The problem was that, even half tuned in, Jessie understood most of what she was saying.

"Isn't it lovely that your grandfather loved Gabe's grandmother so much that he wanted to look after that old coot of a husband she married? There's not a man in a million who'd do that."

Jessie's head began to pound. "That doesn't make it right," she argued. "My grandfather gave away the James future before I was born. And then he let me go on thinking he'd been cheated. I don't think I can forgive him. So many things might have been different if he hadn't. My parents might still be alive." She sighed. "But it doesn't matter now."

"Sometimes a man loves the wrong woman. And when he loves her, he wants to protect her, like Alston protected Martha, like Gabe tried to protect you," Jane defended them.

Jessie couldn't hold back a scoff. "Gabe? The St. Clairs have been after an easement across my land since I was eighteen. Now, they've got it, and Gabe got it for them."

"Then tell me why old Buck St. Clair is going to sell."

"Says who?"

"Lonnie heard it in the barbershop. None of the children want to stay on the mountain. You already know that Walter is looking for a buyer. Now, Buck's decided to sell it all and divide up the money."

It was too much to try to figure out. All Jessie could think about was getting through the governor's dinner and getting back to Dahlonega.

By early afternoon she was ensconced in one of the guest bedrooms in Alice Magadan's luxury mansion. She'd taken a shower, swallowed one of Jane's headache potions, and lain down for a quick nap.

A fleeting longing for the peace and quiet of Pumpkinvine Mountain swept over her. Another night and she'd be back home. But there was no comfort in thinking of the mountain anymore. Everything had changed. It was time she stopped looking for places of peace and made some of her own. Gabe had been right about one thing: A person made her own road.

Just as she drifted off into sleep, she decided to sell Gabe the entire strip. She'd visit it one last time. She'd be saying good-bye to the mountain, just as she'd be saying good-bye to Gabe.

That would tie up all the loose ends. Except one.

What had happened to Horace?

Jessie felt like the biggest fool in Lumpkin County. Here she was, going to the governor's house for dinner, where she'd have to face the most embarrassing moment any James had ever endured, facing the man she'd almost hoodwinked.

Why hadn't she refused? Why on earth would he want to have someone in the mansion whose grandfather had lied? Why on earth was she going with Gabe St. Clair?

The dress Alice had brought from the thrift shop down at the homeless center was a simple gold tunic with a pleated skirt and a gold belt. It was scandalously short, shorter than anything Jessie had worn, except for her dance-hall-girl costume. There were matching gold shoes and a pair of simple gold hoop earrings. Jessie had simply pulled her hair back and caught it with a jeweled clasp, letting it cascade across her shoulders in a raven mass of fine curls.

She was studying herself in the mirror when she heard a quick knock on the door, followed by the sound of it being opened, and a low whistle. It was Gabe.

"Wow! You look spectacular, Jess."

"I feel like an idiot, like a lamb being led to the slaughter. I don't belong here, Gabe. Please, couldn't you explain to the governor and let me go home?"

"Jessie, the governor is very excited that you're coming to dinner. You know that he's a big country music fan. I wouldn't be surprised if he asked you to sing afterward."

"Oh sure," she said in a resigned voice. "I'll give him a rousing rendition of 'Clementine'. After all, I'm a miner's daughter. I don't suppose you have a couple of boxes I could wear, do you?"

"Don't you have any idea how beautiful you are?"

Gabe walked into the room and stood, drinking in the sight of the woman he'd thought he'd left behind. He'd been wrong. Looking at her satiny skin and silky black hair, he couldn't justify his foolish attempt to forget about her. He didn't know why he'd ever tried. There was something proud about her, proud and determined. She was loyal and faithful. She'd spent her life trying to rebuild what she thought her grandfather had lost, only to find that he'd lied about half his fortune and given the rest away.

Such a contradiction.

Just like Jessie.

The dress she was wearing was a statement of the woman. Its golden color was somehow symbolic. The simple cut of the garment was unpretentious, understated. He couldn't take his eyes off the woman he'd once tried to relegate to the status of the pesky hero-worshiper.

"I know I'm like a fish out of water here, Gabe. I'm an outlaw, remember, the last member of the James Gang."

She raised her eyes and allowed herself to look at him standing there in a room so elegant that Jessie had felt like an intruder. Gabe belonged here. His dark suit and highly polished shoes belonged in a place like this. Even his tie was special. It was gold, with a tiny black pattern that complemented both his cream-colored shirt and his gold-streaked hair.

"We look as if we selected matching clothes," he said in amusement.

"Yeah, Barbie and Ken, except Barbie isn't blond."

Gabe took her by the hand and turned her to the mirror over the elaborate marble mantel. "Not Barbie and Ken," he said in a hoarse voice, "an angel and an outlaw."

Jessie didn't want to look. She didn't want to see the two strangers in the mirror. She didn't know those two people. They'd taken over Jessie's and Gabe's bodies and changed them forever.

She took a deep, uneven breath. "Which do you think is which?"

"I think, beautiful lady, that each of us is a little of both. I see here a beautiful angel who has tried to erase her grandfather's mistakes, and a bullheaded outlaw who thought she was trying to conceal them."

"You're wrong, Gabe. What you see is an outlaw who was determined to expose her grandfather's enemies as cheats and thieves. They weren't. All the time they were in the right, and it's time I faced that painful truth."

"We were both wrong about our families, Jessie. But you know, I'm not sure any of that matters. I think they'd all say that it's who we are now that matters."

"Oh, and who is that, Gabe?"

"Just look in the mirror. This is who we are now, Jessie. You don't have to go back to Dahlonega. You can stay here, with me. I'll look after you. I'll make it all up to you."

The truth was in his eyes. He really believed what he was seeing, what he was saying. But the woman in the gold dress wasn't Jessie James. Jessie didn't know who she was, and she wasn't sure she wanted to find out.

Gabe held out his arm. "Shall we go to the ball, Cinderella?"

Jessie might have turned and run, except for Jane's whirlwind entrance. The slight, dark-haired woman was wearing harem pants and a jeweled jacket that might have come straight out of a fairy tale. Behind her, Lonnie, dressed in a simple dark suit, was beaming from ear to ear.

"Oh, my goodness, Jessie, you look good enough to crow about."

"A shining example of a flapdoodle hen, Lonnie, I told you so. She's perfect. We're all perfect. Bring the limo around."

"Limo?" Gabe questioned in amusement as his hand found the small of Jessie's back and pushed her forward. "I thought for sure we'd either be traveling on a Greyhound bus or a magic carpet."

—◆———————◆—

The governor's mansion was a splendid example of Georgian architecture. Tonight it was lit up like a bright jewel in the October evening.

At the entrance, iron gates were opened wide, allowing the limo to pull in and stop at the security station where they were checked, identified, and motioned through. The driver let them out at the front door, then arranged to return for them in two hours.

"Don't know that we'll be ready to go," Jane said, "but if not, you can just sit and wait."

Jessie tried desperately to swallow the lump in her throat. She was more convinced than ever that this was a mistake. This was not the Gold Dust Saloon, and she didn't belong here. Until the governor let out a holler and greeted her with a big smile and a bigger hug.

"Come in, Jessie. This is my wife, Regina. We're so glad you decided to join us. Come on in and meet some of my friends. When I found out you were into country music, I was sorry we didn't have anybody special in town I could invite."

Before she realized what was happening, she was encircled by people who might have been customers in her own saloon. The governor was just a good ole country boy, wearing a three-hundred-dollar suit and cowboy boots. His wife,

Regina, quietly went about making the guests feel welcome and involved in the evening.

Dinner was simple food, soup, salad, roast beef, potatoes, beans, and bread. And the governor was not only an amusing host but well versed in the music industry as well.

By the time dinner was over, Jessie had lost the last of her fears. If she could only lose the shoes that were rubbing a blister on her heel, she might survive her foray into society.

"Now," the governor was saying, "I understand you sing. I know how people are about playing their own instruments, but I do have a couple of guitars around, and I thought we could entertain the folks with a couple of songs, if you wouldn't mind an amateur joining in."

"Governor, I'm an amateur," she protested. "I'm sure these people would rather just talk or something."

But it was soon clear that what the other guests would like was singularly unimportant to their hosts. He wanted to play and sing, and Jessie was going to have to join him. He handed her a guitar far more expensive than anything she'd ever owned.

"It was a gift," he explained, "from Travis Tritt. He lives in Georgia, you know."

"Yes," Jessie said, fingering the strands, checking the tuning. When the governor led off with a spirited rendition of "Clementine," she couldn't hold back her smile. Gabe lifted his shoulders and shook his head, indicating that it wasn't his idea.

An hour later she was enjoying herself. She'd kicked off the shoes and was sitting on a stool singing alone. The governor had laid down his guitar and was listening intently, his foot keeping time with the music.

Without thinking, she eased into the song she'd sang that night when Gabe had come to her club.

> *"Now I'm that woman inside of me.*
> *Yesterday's love has broken free. . . .*
> *And I'm going crazy. . . ."*

She'd lost Gabe in the shadows. Now, she found him, caught his gaze with hers, and stayed with him as she finished the last breathless words.

As applause broke out, she jerked her attention back to the present. "Thank you," she said softly. "It was a pleasure to play with you, Governor."

"No indeed, it was my pleasure, Miss James. And one day, when you're a very famous lady, I'll be able to say once you sang with me."

"Jessie, I'm sorry to interrupt, but we have something of a problem." It was Gabe, holding out her shoes and lifting her to her feet. "If you'll excuse us, Governor."

There was something urgent in Gabe's voice. Jessie didn't argue. "What's wrong?" she asked as they reached the entrance hall.

"It's Horace."

"What's wrong with Horace?"

"He's been taken to the county shelter."

Gabe signaled the limo driver and helped Jessie inside. He gave directions to the driver and leaned back against the seat as the long vehicle glided away.

"Oh, Gabe. How'd you find out?"

"Ben called the mansion. He heard about it. Seems the entire downtown area of Atlanta heard about the mule who made off with a carriage full of tourists and took them to one of the city parks."

"Oh, no! I should have gone with him. Jane told me he was silly about Daisy."

"You mean you knew all about what he was planning?" Gabe was stunned. "How? I mean, how could you, or Jane, possibly know what a mule had in mind?"

"I didn't," Jessie said. "Horace told Jane what he was going to do."

"Why didn't you warn somebody?" Gabe asked as he began to rehearse what he'd tell the press.

"Jane swore me to secrecy."

Gabe could only shake his head. He'd already surmised that Jane was at the bottom of most of the mischief that had happened during the last week. She'd obviously called in the tip that the gold train would be held up. Then, somehow, she and Alice Magadan had cooked up the request for Gabe to ride shotgun to protect the gold. Then followed up with warning notes.

Then he'd compounded the issue by enlisting Jane in the heisting of Jessie's gold.

Now, after making his excuses to the governor, he was on his way to bail out a mule.

The shelter was closed. The fence was locked. If there was an attendant on duty, he refused to answer the door. But Horace knew they were there. He'd come to the fence and announced his displeasure vigorously.

"Hush, Horace!" Jessie said. "Don't alert the law. We're here to break you out!"

"No, we aren't," Gabe disagreed. "We'll come back in the morning and pay his fine like any normal, self-respecting citizen should do."

"And what about Daisy? Horace is in love with her, and if we wait until morning, her owner will claim her."

"As well he should. Daisy belongs to someone else," Gabe said.

At the sound of her name a white horse wearing a straw hat over one ear came shyly

to the fence beside Horace and nickered softly.

"Oh, aren't you a pretty thing," Jessie said,
petting Daisy through the wire. "Horace, I can
see why you were desperate."

"Desperate enough to kidnap a carriage filled
with tourists," Gabe added in a stern voice. "Let's
go, Jess. I promise, I'll be back first thing in
the morning and see what I can do about the
situation."

"But, Gabe—"

"Tomorrow! Good night, Horace. Daisy. Behave yourselves until I get back, please."

Gabe couldn't tell who was the most noncom-
mittal, Horace or Jessie. Back at the Magadan
mansion, Gabe walked Jessie to the door. "I'd
come in, but I'd better get the limo back to the
mansion for Jane and Lonnie. Try not to worry.
Everything will work out, I promise."

"I'm glad you're not betting, Gabe," Jessie said
wearily. "I'm not sure who would win."

"Jessie, wait." Gabe took a step back inside the
door, caught Jessie's hands, and pulled her close.
"I know that things have been . . . unsettled, but I
want you to know that this weekend has been—"

She surprised herself by saying, "Special? I
know."

When he kissed her, his touch was gentle,
reassuring, and a little sad. She leaned against

him for just a moment, allowing herself to enjoy the closeness, then pulled away.

"But the ball is over, Prince Charming. It's almost midnight and if I don't hurry, I'll turn into a scullery maid, and you'll turn into a . . . rat."

"You're mixing your stories, Jessie. We're talking about outlaws and angels here."

"I know you're trying, but you're not my guardian angel, Gabe. I have to look after myself, just as I always have."

Jessie might consider herself a scullery maid, but to Gabe she was a brown-eyed princess. And he was her guardian angel, at least for now, until he figured out an answer to the mess. He could certainly sympathize with Horace. He couldn't be blamed for going after Daisy. His brown eyes were just as disappointed as Jessie's had been when they'd walked away.

"Damn all of you St. Clairs and Jameses. Why couldn't you have been friends?"

It was almost twelve when he deposited Jane and Lonnie at the house, reclaimed his company car, and drove away. Jessie might not be a princess, but he couldn't help feeling like a rat.

NINE

Jessie was dressed in jeans and a football jersey and waiting by the door when Jane and Lonnie returned from the governor's dinner.

"Quick, Jane, change your clothes. We have to rescue Horace and Daisy."

"Gabe told me what happened," Lonnie said. "He's going after them in the morning."

Jessie hurried them up the stairs. "That won't do. Daisy's owner will never let her go with Horace."

"She's right, Lonnie," Jane agreed. "That poor horse has been mistreated terribly. You get the car. I'll get into my working clothes."

"What good will it do to get the car? We can't put a horse and a mule in it. Besides, they still hang you for horse stealing in this state." Lonnie was accustomed to being the practical one, if such a thing could exist around Jane.

"We have friends in high places, Lonnie. Just go! Jane and I will figure it out."

Moments later, wearing a brown trench coat and slacks, Jane was following Jessie down the stairs. "How do we break them out?"

"I've got some wire cutters," Jessie said, "lifted them from the greenhouse out back. We'll cut the lock, let them out, and—and—we'll ride them back here. How's that?"

Jane climbed in the car, nodding as she directed Lonnie. "Sounds good to me. Always did think that garage would make a good stable. In the meantime Lonnie can rent us a couple of horse movers, and we'll get them back to Dahlonega."

"Uh-huh," Lonnie commented, "and what makes you think that the law won't be waiting for you?"

Jessie's frown was one of incredulity. "At the county shelter?"

Lonnie drove quickly toward the older section of downtown Atlanta, where the Animal Control Shelter was located. "No, at the county line. My guess is that Gabe will put two and two together real quick. He's an officer of the law. He isn't going along with you two outlaws breaking it."

"When the time comes to handle Gabe, we'll handle him," Jane promised.

Lonnie gave his wife a long, serious look. "Honey, I don't think you understand Gabriel St. Clair quite as well as you think. He's a man accustomed to giving orders and having them followed. Jessie already has him turned inside out, and this is going to make things worse."

"Don't worry about Gabe, Lonnie," Jessie said with more confidence than she felt. "I've always been able to talk him into something and make him think it was his idea. It's only the people who don't understand his need to control who get in trouble."

Lonnie snorted. "And you do?"

"Of course I do. Now, let's hurry. I've got a bad feeling about this."

Jessie considered Lonnie's warning. He was right. And that was one of the things bothering her. There'd been a time when Gabe would have been in complete accord with her need to bust out the fugitives. The old Gabe would have driven the limo through the fence if that's what it took.

Not this new Gabe.

He was a GBI man now, serious, reserved. And that translated into giving orders and having them followed, something she'd never done and probably couldn't, even if she tried. She wasn't even certain that she liked Gabe's new reserve. That new quality had cost him something. He'd lost his flare for the dramatic, his ability to live on the edge. The truth was staring Jessie in the face, and it had been from the beginning.

The Gabe who'd come to be her guardian angel wasn't the Gabe who'd run wild with her through their childhood. He'd changed and adjusted to life, while she'd fought it every step of the way. Maybe she was wrong, but she didn't think that she was very different. Life was a challenge, nothing came easy, and she was still spitting trouble in the eye, scrapping for everything she wanted. Even her saloon was a statement. She could have opened a restaurant and probably done just as well. At least most of her income wouldn't go for upkeep and salaries.

But there would have been no excitement in mashed potatoes and meat loaf. Not one resident of Dahlonega would have scratched his head at what Jessie James was doing if she'd opted for a tearoom. That would have been too calm, boring. She was the same outlaw she'd always been. Jessie took her heritage seriously. Her grandfather had scoffed at being a normal breadwinner. A gold miner was what he was and what he remained for all his life, even if there was no more gold on James land.

No matter how honest she was about the rest, there was one thing that hadn't changed—the electricity that arced between her and Gabe, the fierce need to touch and be close, to share their deepest emotions. She thought that Gabe was falling in love with her, and it scared her. Always before it had been her in pursuit of him. Now, they were in foreign territory. The very thing she'd always hoped for was the thing that was pushing them apart.

How did an outlaw and an angel find common ground, and could they survive their differences if they did?

Jessie let out a deep sigh.

"What's wrong, girl?"

"I don't know. There are times when I wonder why I worry so much about things nobody else seems to care about."

"Because you're Jessie James, and you understand about pain and suffering," Jane said with authority. "You attack it, subdue it, and move on to the next moment."

"But this time I seem to be stuck in the suffering."

"No," Lonnie contradicted. "You just think you have to play the role of the outlaw like your grandfather set you up to do. What about your father, didn't he ever sit you down and tell you about how normal folks get things done?"

"My father was just as impractical, Lonnie, in a different way. He was a dreamer who thought the world was a cruel place. He wanted to live a simple life, and nobody would let him do it."

"Uh-huh," Lonnie said quietly. "Folks have told me about your father's simple life. In my time that translated to being shiftless and irresponsible."

"Lonnie!" Jane gave her husband an uncharacteristic slap on the shoulder. "You don't know what happened to the man to cause him to retreat. He'd lost the life he knew and the woman he loved."

"Yeah, and he had a child. He ought to have accepted his responsibility and made a home for her. That's what Gabe would do."

Yes, Jessie thought. That was what Gabe would do. But what about her? Could she accept being someone's responsibility? She'd always told herself that if Pop hadn't died—if her father hadn't been killed—if her mother had lived. . . .

They'd all left. But Jessie made up her mind that she wouldn't go. If she bought back the land, it would be like recovering pieces of herself. But instead of reclaiming it, she was in danger of losing it all. Maybe it was time. Maybe Gabe had been right all along. Now, she was into maybes, and he was the one who was sure.

"Jane," she began, looking for something to take her mind off Gabe and the mountain. "About that attempt to steal the gold, it was you that phoned in the tip, wasn't it?"

"Of course it was," Lonnie answered for her. "She had some fool idea that it would publicize Gold Rush Days, and everybody would benefit."

Jessie had to ask, though she wasn't sure she wanted to hear the answer. "Was it because of you that Gabe came back?"

"Well . . ." Jane was delaying, an action that seemed out of character.

"I want to know the truth, Jane."

"Yes and no," she finally said. "I didn't know Gabe personally, but I did know about Gabe and you, about the relationship that you'd had as children. Gavin told me."

"And how did Gavin know?"

"Gabe and Gavin Magadan were friends. Before Gavin married, Gabe would come home with him now and then. He'd talk to Alice with such poignancy about that mountain and you. Then when I learned—no, let me put it this way. After Lonnie and I came to Dahlonega and decided to stay, I saw how lonely you were."

"And the two busiest bodies in Atlanta couldn't bear it," Lonnie said with unconcealed pride. "She and Alice plotted to do something to get Gabe back up there. When you decided to bring the gold to town, Alice came up with the idea. With those two women's connections Gabe never had a chance."

"But I already knew it was meant to be," Jane said confidently, "I saw it in the cards."

Lonnie gave out an exclamation of resignation.

"Well, it almost worked," Jane insisted.

And it had almost worked, Jessie admitted to herself, if not to her two companions in crime. Except she was the outlaw, and Gabe had gone straight. Still, they might have had a chance, except for the gold. Now she owed Gabe, and that changed everything. Nothing would be through choice anymore.

Ah, Pops, looks as if what goes around comes around. You rescued and provided for Martha St. Clair because you cared for her. Now, Gabe is rescuing and providing for me because he cares. And both of your efforts have cost you the women who love you.

Lonnie pulled into the parking area of the animal shelter and cut the engine. The lights, still burning, settled on Horace and Daisy, pressed against the fence.

"Cut the lights, Lonnie," Jane said. "Jessie, let's get to it." They stepped out of the car and straight into—

"Gabe?" Jessie blurted out. "What are you doing here?"

"I started home, and then I remembered old man Pendleton's watermelons, and I knew what you'd do. So I decided to wait."

"Oh, Gabe. You came to help," Jessie couldn't keep the pleasure from her voice.

"No, I came to stop you. Take Jane home, Lonnie. I'll deal with Jessie."

Once Lonnie drove away, Jessie headed to the fence and hooked the wire cutters around the lock.

"Jessie, I don't think you want to do that."

"Of course I do. We'll ride Horace and Daisy back to Jane's house, and you can come back for your car. Oh, Gabe, it's just like old times, you and me, outwitting the law."

He didn't have the heart to remind her that he was the law. And it felt good to do something together as they once had. Throwing caution to the winds, he took the cutters and went to work.

They almost made it. The lock had been cut on the gate, and Jessie had slipped inside when the siren sounded.

"We've been found out, Jessie," Gabe shouted. "Let's make a run for it!"

Jessie vaulted onto Horace's back and started through the gate with Daisy falling in behind. But a cordon of black-and-white police cars with whirling blue lights quickly blocked their escape. Gabe didn't even try to get away. He simply walked forward, holding up his arms.

Her throat tight with disappointment, Jessie slid off Horace's back and led the mule back inside.

"Sorry, old boy. I tried. Looks like you'll have to wait till morning."

"What do you think you're doing?" the first officer on the scene asked.

"Breaking these innocent animals out of jail," Jessie said, "and we could have, if you boys had been five minutes later. Who tipped you off?"

The officers looked at each other in amazement.

"You're staging a breakout for a mule and a horse?" the second man in blue asked.

"We were," Gabe answered, resigned for the worst. He was certain that the headlines of the morning newspaper would read LOCAL GBI AGENT ARRESTED FOR MULE-NAPPING.

The officer took a good look at Gabe. "What's your name, son?"

"Gabriel St. Clair."

"Didn't I see you on the news today, down at the capitol with that gold train?"

"You did."

The officer turned to Jessie. "And you, ma'am?"

"Who else?" she said in resignation. "You've captured Jessie James."

They were handcuffed and placed in the backseat of the squad car. Instead of being concerned, Jessie had a grin planted across her face that didn't waver.

Gabe couldn't believe what he'd done. "I don't understand why you're so happy," he finally said. "Didn't this weekend suggest anything to you?"

"Yes, it told me that together we're as unstoppable as heat lightning in July."

"Oh, Jess. That's what I'm afraid of." What he didn't say was that it scared the hell out of him how easy it had been for him to become ensnared by her spirit again. For ten years he'd distanced himself from that temptation by avoiding the mountain. Now, in one weekend, he'd jeopardized everything he'd worked for.

The resignation in Gabe's voice killed her rush of enthusiasm.

"I'm sorry, Gabe. I didn't think. . . ."

That was Jessie's trouble. She never stopped to think. She operated strictly on feelings. He stifled his feelings and relied on rational thought processes.

Until tonight.

But, dammit, back there with Jessie, he felt more alive than he had in years. For a moment he understood the high a criminal must feel in the midst of a crime.

"Gabe, I'll tell them it was me. You were there officially, trying to stop me."

"It won't work. I wasn't stopping you."

"Honestly, Gabe, you are the most stubborn person I've ever met. You analyze life too much. Just give in to your feelings and let them carry you."

"Stubborn? Yes, I am. I'm also a realist. The problem in trying to have a relationship with you is that it's all or nothing."

"Aren't they always?"

"Maybe, but you'd be like a fish out of water here, and I—I don't think I can go back to the mountain. Now, after this, I'll probably lose my job and be right back where I was."

"Be quiet back there," the officer yelled.

They were taken to the police station. When the arresting officer identified his prisoners, they were told to have a seat in a waiting area while Ben Jansen was notified. Jessie sat with her elbows on her knees and her chin resting on her hands as she looked around.

"I'm truly sorry, Gabe. I guess I've gotten you into trouble. I'm used to it, but this is your territory, and I was wrong. What can I do?"

"Don't do anything," said Gabe, trying to decide how he was going to explain his irrational behavior to his superior officer.

"On the other hand, we are being arrested. Too bad we can't turn this into a real happening. You know," she mused, springing to her feet as she talked, "we could use this to accomplish some good."

"Forget it, Jessie," Gabe said in a tense voice. "I'm all out of happenings. I'm hungry. I'm dirty. I've probably lost my job, and I'm not in the mood for a safari, a protest, or a barn burning."

"No, listen to me. What if we say we were staging a breakout to publicize the plight of incarcerated animals? The newspapers would like that."

"Oh, yes. But I doubt the governor would. We've obliterated his public-relations venture for Gold Rush Days, to say nothing of my future as a GBI agent."

"Incarcerated animals?" one of the women waiting repeated incredulously. "You're worried about animals? What about incarcerated people, or those about to be?"

"But people have a choice," Jessie argued. "Horace didn't. What were you arrested for?"

"Offering to make a man happy. Can you imagine, he picked me up, and they arrested him too." At Jessie's confused expression the woman expounded, "Look, lady, I'm a hooker."

Jessie started to laugh. "You won't believe this, but that's how we ended up here."

"You two are hookers?"

"No, but we have a friend, Horace, who picked up a—never mind, you won't believe it. But people have rights, animals don't. We could make a statement. What do you say, Gabe?"

But Gabe just sat. All he could think about was that in spite of the publicity of his possible reprimand, probably even the loss of his job, he and Jessie were a team again. They weren't on the mountain now, and they weren't kids. Still, it felt right. Jessie was always ready to follow her heart's feelings, and he was only now learning that his could feel. And that was what was bothering the hell out of him.

"Gabe?" she repeated. "What do you say?"

"I say, let Horace and Daisy enjoy their relationship for as long as they can. Ours may never survive the publicity we're about to generate."

"Oh, you're saying we have a relationship? Good. I've never heard you admit it before. Why don't we figure out how we're going to handle this when Ben gets here."

They didn't have to worry about handling anything. The arrival of Miss Emily Moran and her cameraman took care of that.

"Is it true?" she asked, microphone in hand. "Have you been arrested?"

"We have been," Jessie admitted.

"For what?" The TV camera was focused on Jessie and Gabe.

"Breaking and entering, and theft," she answered, taking Gabe's arm and smiling into the camera. "Though I prefer calling it kidnapping."

"Who told you?" Gabe asked.

"I have my sources," the reporter answered. "Who did you kidnap?"

"Horace and Daisy," Jessie answered, "they—"

Gabe cut her off. "I don't suppose I could convince you to forget about this story, Miss Moran."

"Not a chance."

That was the moment Ben arrived, brushing the reporter aside with a "No Comment" as he took Jessie's arm and hustled her through a door that took them into the back and out into the parking garage.

"What's all this about, Gabe?" he asked as they were escorted to a waiting car.

Gabe gave a brief, unadorned explanation of the evening, making no excuse for his involvement. He knew it wouldn't have mattered. From the grim set of Ben's face Gabe knew he was about to become unemployed at a time when he needed money to help Jessie. Maybe selling the St. Clair mountain land was going to turn into a blessing.

"You aren't going to fire Gabe, are you, Mr. Jansen?"

"It may not be up to me. The bureau has a strict code of conduct for its employees, and breaking and entering is against state law."

"Actually," Jessie said helpfully, "it's worse. Horse stealing is still a hanging offense."

"We didn't steal the horse, we only made the attempt," Gabe corrected.

Ben took a deep, calming breath before he commented. "Horse stealing, breaking and entering. You couldn't just do it quietly—you had to conduct an interview with the press, complete with pictures."

He drove Jessie back to the Magadans and left instructions with Jane and Alice that she wasn't to be allowed to leave. "You," he said to Gabe, "I'll deal with you after I've checked with the governor."

"Oh, Jane, I'm afraid I've really done it this time. Gabe's in trouble, and it's all my fault."

"Gabe's a big boy," Lonnie commented as he closed the door behind her. "He'll take care of himself. He always has."

"But he wouldn't be in trouble if I hadn't talked him into helping me. Then he wouldn't let me take the blame. He thinks he's got to protect me, the way he did when he had you steal the gold and then later when he offered to buy that easement; all so that I wouldn't be exposed as a liar. I've really done it, haven't I?"

Jane put her arm around Jessie. "I doubt you could talk Gabe into doing anything he didn't want to do. I suspect you never did. Come and have some cocoa and tell me all about it."

When she'd heard the story, Jane began to

pace. "I have it. I'll give the shelter a call first thing in the morning. I'm sure a large donation will make them drop the matter. And with the governor interceding with the police, you'll be fine."

But the pleasure Jessie had felt having Gabe beside her had begun to recede in the face of reality. Gabe's future was the important issue. Gabe was kind and generous, and he didn't deserve what had happened. She loved him too much to see him lose the future he'd worked so hard for. And this time she couldn't see a way she could make things right.

She was waiting in the breakfast room the next morning when Gabe arrived. Jane and Lonnie had disappeared on some mysterious errand. Gabe's serious expression said louder than words that the situation was grim.

"What's the verdict, Gabe?" she asked, then crossed her fingers behind her back and made a wish that she'd disappear from the earth.

"The judge heard the story and took the governor's recommendation. The charges have been dropped against Jessie James—with one condition."

"What?"

"That you be remanded into my custody for a period of one year, during which you will perform free of charge for any and all charities that wish to make use of your talents."

"No, I mean what about you, Gabe? Did Ben fire you?"

"It's up to me. If I stay, I'll likely be reassigned to a less visible location. What that means is that I'll be hidden while I'm in disgrace."

"Where?"

"I don't know yet. Can I trust you, Jessie?" Gabe asked, pinning her down with the intensity of his gaze. "To come along quietly, to behave yourself if I vouch for you while you're in my custody?"

"Your custody? If you vouch for me?" There was the beginning of a smile on her face. "Does this mean that I'll have to answer to you?"

"It does!" Gabe agreed sternly.

"Well, I don't know," she said. "Why should I?"

"Because I— Dammit to hell, Jess, when are you going to stop fighting me? This is serious. I can't promise you anything, and I don't know what I'm going to do. All I know is that I want to be with you."

There might have been only the two of them, standing nose-to-nose, eyes flashing, lips trembling. They set off such waves of electricity that cook, who'd started to answer the door, backed away without speaking.

"What about my mountain, Gabe? Will I be able to survive if I leave it?"

"I don't expect you to leave."

"But you won't be happy there, and I might do something to disappoint you. I'll always push you into doing things you ought not to do."

"Then I'll put you under house arrest."

"You wouldn't dare," she said softly.

"Only if you push and push and make me so angry that all I want to do is tie you in a knot."

"And you don't tie me in knots? I couldn't be tied any tighter than I am right now, Gabe."

"Nor could I," he admitted, closing the space between them to a tantalizing matter of inches. "Ah, Jess. I'm in love with you. What in hell are we going to do?"

His lips brushed hers lightly, hovering like some powerful winged creature drawing nourishment from the center of the forbidden flower before settling possessively.

She ought to push him away, she thought as her lips parted beneath his and a shudder swept through her, buckling her knees. Only Gabe's strong arms kept her from crumpling to the floor. After a long moment Gabe dragged himself back, looking down at Jessie with eyes heavy with desire.

"Let's get out of here, outlaw," he said.

"Are you sure you want me, Gabe?"

"I'm sure. God help us both, but I'm sure."

❧━━━━━━━━━❧

By telephone Walter agreed to Jane's offer to buy the farm. Lonnie's mysterious task was to buy Daisy from the owner of the carriage stand and arrange transporting the animals back to their new quarters in the pasture on Walter's land at the base of Pumpkinvine Mountain.

The story of Horace and Daisy made Emily Moran's *News at Noon*, along with pictures of Jane and Lonnie, who turned the event into a plea for the adoption of animals who had so much love to give.

There was no mention on the news of Jessie and Gabe, but they wouldn't have known if they'd been the lead story. They were headed back to Dahlonega, Gabe grinning like a Cheshire cat and Jessie humming a fractured version of "Clementine." There were still unsolvable problems between them. But for now, both put them aside.

They were experienced in snatching moments of pleasure; their entire relationship had been built on privacy, and could never survive the pressure of the outside world. As children they'd hidden in the woods. As teens they'd kept the true closeness of their relationship secret. As adults they'd accepted that they were two ships that passed in the night.

Gabe stopped only once, for gas at a trucker's stop on the outskirts of Atlanta. He didn't talk, and neither did Jessie. They were simply together, the memory of their kiss still burning their lips with its potency and their bodies with its promise.

When Gabe turned into the entrance to the Lake Lanier campgrounds where they'd stopped on the way to Atlanta, Jessie cast a quizzical eye.

"I left something here, I think," Gabe said. "I wanted to come back and be sure. Do you mind?"

"No, I suppose not. Except Nathan must be wondering what happened to me. I do have a business to run."

"Nathan is fine. I checked. He isn't expecting you until tomorrow."

"Tomorrow?"

Gabe drove the Jeep to the spot beneath the trees by the lake and cut the engine. He got out, moved to the back, and removed a basket and a blanket, then strode purposefully toward the lake beyond the road.

Jessie scrambled after him.

"What do you mean telling Nathan I won't be there until tomorrow? I . . ."

Gabe stopped, dropped the basket and the blanket, and pulled her into his arms.

" . . . have a business to run, and it's my decision when and what I—"

"Shut up, Jessie!" he rasped out, swallowing her protest as he kissed her.

All reason fled from her mind, as always when Gabe wrapped her in his arms. She tried to muster up enough strength of will to push him away, tried, even as her muscles were turning to mush. She'd always known that Gabe was stronger, but strength was not the issue. With little resistance her body molded itself to him. Her lips parted, and she returned every movement.

A frisson of heat ran down her spine, radiating outward to burn away any suggestion of resistance. Jessie moaned, twisting, burrowing herself against him. She was his with no effort.

And Gabe knew it. It had always been that way. Not with kisses in the beginning, but with smiles, shared treasures, then words and dreams. Now, all those things were woven together into the snare, and they'd been caught in it.

Both were lost in the heat of the moment, the feeling of goodness that erupted from hands that touched and breath that mingled between kisses and soft murmurs of desire. And then they were on the ground, clothing gone before either knew that it had been discarded.

He opened his eyes, finding that she was watching his chest. He must have sighed for eyelids heavy with the dazed look of uncontrolled need lifted, revealing dark eyes, wicked eyes, eyes that simmered and asked.

"Jessie?"

"Please, Gabe. Don't stop now."

"Ah, Jessie." He groaned as he moved over her. "You make me crazy. Crazy!"

"No," she whispered, lifting her hips to take him, *yesterday's love has broken free*. That's 'Jessie's Song.' "

TEN

They spent the night under the stars, neither thinking about tomorrow.

Reality returned the next morning as they drove back to Lumpkin County. They hadn't found any answers, they'd just made more questions. The closer they got to Dahlonega, the quieter Jessie became. When the mountain came into view, she let out an involuntary sigh of contentment.

That sigh was his answer. He couldn't drop Jessie and drive away. Telling her that he loved her didn't make things right. She wouldn't pack her bags and come back to Atlanta with him, and even though he no longer felt the desperate need to be away from Pumpkinvine Mountain, he wasn't sure he was ready to live in Dahlonega.

The only difference between his situation now and the other times he'd left Jessie was that now he admitted to himself that he was in love with her. Nothing else had changed.

He wasn't even sure what would "make things right."

"What do we do now, Jessie?" he finally said.

"Do? Get on with our lives, I suppose."

She didn't know what she'd expected him to say. Until he got his new assignment, he wouldn't know where he was going. She still needed her place, and he still didn't feel comfortable sharing it. They were long past the time when he'd lay his head in her lap and talk through his problems. She couldn't look at him. She had to be strong. If she caught sight of those flashing blue eyes, she'd start to cry, and Jessie James was too tough for tears.

"I'll stay out of trouble, Gabe. I won't embarrass you anymore."

He took a long, deep breath. "You think it will be that easy?" *Leaving you?*

"No, I don't. I don't think it will be easy at all." *Don't go.* "But it has to be done." She wasn't even sure what "it" was.

Desperately, Jessie looked through the windows at the hazy shapes of the mountains in the distance. There was something beautifully sad and romantic about the clouds that hung low across the peaks like pastel finger marks of blue. They were smeared as if they were filled with water.

When she was little, her father had said the clouds were crying. He'd said the whole world was crying inside, some people simply hid it better than others.

She tried not to feel the swell in her throat that was making it more difficult to swallow. The closer they came to Dahlonega, the grayer the sky turned, as if even the elements sensed that the end was near.

"I don't think I can walk away and leave you again," Gabe said in a tight voice. "I don't want to say good-bye."

"I know," she whispered. "It isn't your fault, Gabe. We're both flawed, and the mountain has become our excuse."

"Isn't love enough?" he asked.

"It wasn't for our parents. We're the only ones left, Gabe. Do you think that we're afraid of change?"

"Have I ever asked you to change, Jess?"

She didn't answer.

He persisted. "Don't you understand that you're the part of me that reaches out and grabs for the brass ring? I finally understand that, and I'm not sure I can let that go."

She cut her eyes over to him, taking in the furrow of his brow, the firm lips that had taken her to places she'd dreamed of but never expected to go. But it was more than making love with Gabe. If she was the excitement in his life, he was the stability in hers. And she didn't want him to change. She wanted him around.

As if he were analyzing the problem and had found an answer, he nodded. "Maybe it's time we stop holding on to what was and see what might be."

Jessie wanted to agree, but she wasn't sure it would be fair to Gabe. He'd already found out what it meant to belong to her world. They'd been thrown in jail, and his career had been put in danger.

"You're into maybes again," she said. "I don't know. This weekend has pretty much destroyed my perception of what was. I found out that my grandfather, the one person in my life whom I trusted, was in love with another man's wife. He sacrificed our family's future to take care of her, which was gallant, but then he covered it with a lie. The irony was that, after all that, he found— well, it doesn't matter now."

"That's what I mean, Jess. You can't be any more rocked by your discovery than I was to learn that Uncle Buck is courting your church organist and considering leaving the mountain. I can't wait for him to learn that his daddy didn't win the mine fair and square."

"Let's don't tell him, Gabe. What purpose would that serve?"

"It would stop the lies. I don't want any more lies between us, Jessie."

"Why do families lie to their children, Gabe?"

"I think it is an extension of lying to themselves."

"Are we doing that, Gabe?"

He didn't have an answer.

By noon they were stopping in front of the saloon. The sidewalks were already teeming with tourists and cadets from the military college nearby. Across the street the Nugget Hotel had moved some of their tables from the porch down to the sidewalks, where parcel-laden visitors were having lunch and enjoying the festive atmosphere.

"Looks like Jane's advertising campaign worked," Gabe said as he maneuvered the car to a stop.

"I can't believe all these people," Jessie said, viewing the crowds in amazement. "And Gold Rush Days haven't even started yet."

"Too bad her plan for us was a failure."

Jessie turned around to face Gabe. "Don't you dare say that. You came back to help me, and you did. Because of you I can replace the gold my grandfather lied about having. That's important to me."

"I wish I could do more."

"I'm very grateful for what you did, and I'll repay you. I'll find a way." Her voice shook slightly. "I promise!"

She didn't know why she was getting so emotional. Because, she admitted, no matter what he said, Gabe would be leaving. Anytime she and Gabe were together, it was a prelude to goodbye. First there was surprise. Then came joy and excitement, followed by some kind of emotional upheaval, ending in pain and loneliness. She and Gabe seemed always to part angry. This was to be no exception.

"Jessie, darling, you don't owe me anything. I'm paying for something my family has always wanted. You get the money you need, and we get access to the land we need to sell. That brings the last St. Clair down from the mountain, and an era ends."

"No, it's more than that. It ties you to your family again, even if it is only temporary. I appreciate your sacrifice."

"I don't want your gratitude. I want—" Gabe broke off. What the hell did he want? He wanted Jessie, and he had no idea how to make it happen. He turned his head in frustration. "Jane was wrong," he finally said.

"About what?"

"The New Guinea flapdoodle hen. She's not only good at flapping her wings; she's pretty good at doodling too. It's the mating for life that she was wrong about."

"Gabe, I don't know what you're talking about, but I think I'd better get out before the sheriff has to arrest a forty-second cousin for obstructing traffic."

As Jessie got out, Gabe heard car horns blaring impatiently. He looked into his rearview mirror and saw the line of traffic behind him.

Jessie came around the front of the vehicle to his open window and stopped. "I'll get the paperwork drawn up on the land. Where will you be?"

"At the hotel, for a day or so, anyway. I'll make arrangements to get your money."

She lingered.

He let the engine continue to idle.

Neither wanted the morning to end, but neither knew how to justify prolonging it.

Raindrops did what rational thinking and car horns didn't. The downpour splattered the windshield of the Bronco and made wet splotches on Jessie's shirt.

She gave Gabe one last desperate look, then turned and ran into the door being held open by Nathan. She didn't wait to see Gabe pull away. He didn't look back to see if she had.

Inside the Gold Dust it seemed only fitting that Mike, the piano player for the Dusters, was sitting in the darkness, fingering the melody to their song.

I'll have to add a verse. Losing love is worse than going crazy. It's beyond physical pain.

The next day the papers were delivered to Gabe at the hotel.

Gabe read the document and felt a band tighten across his chest. She'd found a way to show her gratitude, too, and end the ongoing bone of contention between the St. Clairs and the Jameses. Instead of granting an easement to the landlocked property as they'd agreed, the papers were a full bill of sale for the strip of land in question.

If he accepted what Jessie was offering, she would no longer own a piece of her beloved mountain, and he would be permanently tied to a past he'd left behind, for he could never sell her land.

There had to be another way. Jessie deserved more, so much more, but he knew that she wouldn't accept less than full payment of her debts. God knew, he didn't want that land. But he wasn't a wealthy man. He'd have to use the last of his football money. No matter how much he'd needed it before, he'd never spent it. It was his security blanket, his ticket out of the mountains. Now, he was about to

spend it on the very thing he'd escaped from—
for Jessie.

He held the contract and thought back to the
fire in Jessie's eyes when they tried to rescue
Horace and Daisy, to the way she responded
to his kisses and to her enduring loyalty to her
family. Jessie was more than special; she was the
only constant in his life. He'd been some kind of
fool for telling himself he didn't need that.

Now that he understood, could he leave without destroying himself? He didn't know.

Finally, in desperation, Gabe exchanged the
company car for his Jeep and headed for the
mountain. It was time he personally inspected
the section of land he was gaining access to.

An hour later he'd gone as far as he could
on the old road. Leaving his vehicle behind, he
continued on foot. There was such beauty on the
mountain. Squirrels chattered in the trees. A bird
gave a raucous call, and the fall leaves crackled
as he strode across them. The higher he got, the
cooler the air, the more lush the evergreens, the
more peaceful the afternoon.

Now and then he'd simply stop and listen,
allowing himself to absorb the odd sensation of
excited expectancy. He'd never come up here
before, not once, in spite of all his uncle's
cajoling and promises that this section of land
would be his.

Now, the higher he got, the stronger the pull. He felt as if there was something, or someone, waiting, and unconsciously he hurried.

He stumbled on the little house by accident, and once he saw it, he understood where he was being drawn. Nestled in the edge of a stand of mountain laurel, mountain pines, and fir was a log cabin. Around its doorway, saucy, late-flowering mountain daisies still bloomed. A carpet of pine needles lay over the ground around the cabin like undisturbed insulation. Tree limbs interwove themselves overhead as if to protect the little house.

He walked around to the rear, where an open porch looked out over the valley below. He felt as if he were on top of the world. Opening the back door was simple; it wasn't locked. Inside, he had the feeling that the room had been left but not abandoned. There was a spirit of expectancy, as if the little cabin had stood waiting.

A chipmunk scurried across the floor, disappearing into a slightly open door that turned out to be a pantry, still stocked with very old canned goods, the labels peeled away. Gabe opened the windows and let the fresh air carry away the musty odors. The odd feeling of expectancy changed into one of warm welcome that surprised him.

Though the natural rock fireplace was laid with logs, an animal had scratched the materials out, probably carrying them off for a nest. There was a rusty iron kettle on the black woodstove. Gabe had the absurd feeling that it was filled with water. Someone had covered the furniture with sheets and faded quilts that had shredded away years before. Amid clouds of dust, Gabe stripped them off, exposing the tattered remains of a couch and a matching chair. Another draped shape turned into a rocker, pulled close to the hearth. A hole in the roof had let in the rain, rotting the wooden chair, allowing one arm to fall to the floor. Vines grew through the cracks and across one wall, draping it in green. Still, with every move, he felt the strange feeling of welcome expand.

This was where his grandmother had come to meet her lover. He knew that; he felt that love. It nudged his skin and fired his blood. Sanctuary, he decided, this was a place where love could be safe. This was a place where demons were cast out and the future was some distant place that paled into insignificance.

Gabe stood in the middle of the room and looked around. This was why Martha had sold all the land around it. So nothing would be disturbed. So her sanctuary would last forever.

He walked over to the small desk by the window and riffled through the paperwork. There was a half-finished note that disintegrated when he touched it, and a book of poetry open and laid facedown.

He lifted it carefully and made out the name—*Maude Muller*. He knew the poem, about star-crossed lovers who'd married the wrong ones and lived quiet, desperate lives dreaming of what might have been.

But the room didn't feel like that. Even the air seemed to exude a kind of glow. The dust caught the light and shimmered, giving the illusion of flecks of swirling gold. Warmth, the visible glow of love, was here, preserved and . . . waiting.

Gabe leaned into the fireplace and saw daylight up the chimney. He took a chance and lit the fire. Soon the cheery flames were licking at the dry logs, sending physical warmth into the cooling October afternoon. He sat down on the couch, propped his feet on the nearby stool, and allowed his mind to roam free.

His grandmother had known love here, and she'd been forced to turn her back on it. But she'd known it, welcomed it in a time when such a thing as an affair would have been grounds for humiliation and the worst kind of censure. But she'd given it up when her husband had returned from the war a sick, broken man. Her choice was made for her.

But his future was still his to choose, as was Jessie's. What he was grudgingly ready to concede was that with all their headstrong decisions about following their own stars, they'd chosen loneliness. Neither of them would ever have what old Alston and Martha had shared. He and Jessie were turning their backs on their feelings without having to, without having known the kind of love this cabin had nurtured.

Sanctuary.

Nurtured.

Gabe was beginning to get an idea. It was too dark to return to his four-wheel drive. He'd spend the night, and tomorrow, tomorrow, he'd explore the idea that was only just forming in his mind.

The signed contract for the land on Pumpkinvine Mountain and the record producer were both at the door waiting for Jessie the next morning when she opened the saloon.

"I've listened to your music," Cullen Marshall said as he followed Jessie back inside. "And I think you have talent."

"Thanks," she said with less enthusiasm than the man obviously expected.

"In fact, I'd like to offer you a record deal. I called, but your associate couldn't give me the name of your agent."

"Agent? I don't have one."

"Well, that isn't necessary. I'm sure we can work out something. We'll bring you to Nashville, where we'll work on choosing the songs and deciding how we'll market you."

She looked at him in disbelief. "Nashville? You'd expect me to move to Nashville?"

"Not permanently, but for a time. There are months of hard work ahead of us before we can record. You'll need to be booked at some of the smaller clubs, to get the feel of going on the road. We'll have to find musicians to back you."

"Mr.—Mr. Marshall, I have no intention of leaving Dahlonega, but if I did sign a contract with you, the Dusters would be the musicians on any record."

"I'm afraid that we'd need people to spotlight you who have a bit more experience, Jessie."

He was patient, speaking as if he were dealing with a ten-year-old, certain that he was in charge and she'd fall in line.

"Then I guess we won't make a deal. Thank you for your offer, but I'll have to refuse. The Dusters may decide to sell you the song, but since Mike wrote the music, I'll leave it up to him."

She was turning him down. The record producer was stunned. "I don't think you understand, Miss James. We're talking about quite a large amount of money."

"Oh? How much?"

"Well, we'd start with an advance of ten thousand dollars. Temporary housing is included, a new wardrobe, transportation, and of course a per diem to take care of expenses."

Ten thousand cash? She looked down at the contract she was still holding, the contract she'd signed agreeing to sell Gabe her land in exchange for money to acquire the gold her grandfather had promised to the state. If she'd waited, she could have earned the money herself. Even if it had meant leaving Lumpkin County, it wouldn't have been forever. And the mountain would still have belonged to her.

But it had come too late.

"Miss James," the producer said, "this is a good offer. I'd advise you to consider it carefully."

"I'm sorry. I'm sure it is. It's just that I don't need it now. I might have left on a temporary basis, never permanently. But," she repeated, "it's too late now."

"But, Jess . . ." Mike stepped forward from the area where the band stored their equipment. "What about us?"

She turned a stricken eye on her old friend. "Oh, Mike, I'm sorry. I—I can't go. But you can. Take the song, record it with someone else."

"I'll take the song, Miss James," Mr. Marshall agreed, "but you have to be a part of the deal."

"Then I'm afraid we don't have a deal," Jessie said. "The only way 'Jessie's Song' will ever be recorded is by the Dusters. I wouldn't consider any other option."

"I'll leave my card," he finally said. "If you change your mind, call me."

She turned back to Mike, hugging him briefly. "I'm sorry, Mike. But he isn't the only producer in country music."

"I know, but he's the only one who's come to hear us. Wonder if that ditzy square-dancer over at the hotel knows any other producers."

"Jane sent him here?"

"According to him." Mike turned back to the piano.

As Jessie walked past the bar and up the stairs to her apartment, she heard him picking out the melody, one note at a time. She'd passed crazy. She was numb.

The banker notified Jessie that the money had been deposited into her account. Jessie contracted with another miner to supply the gold and deliver it to the sheriff, who promised to get it to the governor.

Gold Rush Days got off with a bang. The streets were full from early morning until late at night. The Gold Dust was pulling in a standing-room-only crowd, and the cash registers were jingling. Jessie had to hire extra help, as did

Jane and Lonnie across the street in the Nugget Hotel.

Nobody mentioned Gabe. His Jeep was seen all over Dahlonega for several days, then it disappeared. Jessie assumed that he'd returned to Atlanta. It hurt that he hadn't said good-bye, but it was best. They'd never been much for good-byes in the past, and this one would have been harder.

The band played, and Jessie's hurting songs brought tears to the eyes of her guests. Nathan began to worry about the dark shadows under Jessie's eyes and her loss of appetite. Always before she'd actively intermingled with her guests. Now, when she wasn't working, she stayed in her apartment. He finally broached the subject with Jane, who agreed that it was time that someone intervened.

"You're not going to mess with Jessie's life anymore," Lonnie argued. "This time I'll put my foot down."

"Of course not," Jane agreed sweetly, and called Gabe in Atlanta. "Do you still intend to come back for the final weekend of festivities?"

"I do. I'm working out the plan with Ben Jansen. But I'll be there."

"There's been a new development here," Jane reported, "that record producer wants to record 'Jessie's Song.' He offered her a lot of money."

"What did she say?"

"She turned it down."

Gabe wasn't surprised to hear that Jessie had been offered the record deal, nor was he surprised to learn that she'd turned it down. If she wouldn't leave the mountain to record her songs, why should he expect her to give it up for him? Still, he was determined to carry out his plan.

"I'll see you tomorrow night, Jane," he said. "Tell Horace I'm coming for a visit."

ELEVEN

The grand finale of Gold Rush Days was the crowning of the new Miss Nugget. Leading up to that event, the hog-calling contest had ended and the fiddling had begun. Tourists who'd heard enough earsplitting hollering turned away from the square and surged down the street lined with craft shops, restaurants, the Nugget Hotel, and the Gold Rush Saloon.

Nobody, not even the organizers, expected what happened next.

Over the noise of the crowd and the music came the sound of gunshots. Everyone hushed and looked toward the end of the street where a magnificent black horse, carrying a rider wearing a large black hat and firing a long-barreled pistol into the air, came into view.

The crowd parted, convinced that this was part of the ongoing celebration. The horse came to a stop in front of the saloon, allowing its rider to slide to the ground. After giving a threatening motion to the onlookers, the mean-looking hombre moved inside.

Just as he stepped through the doorway, Jessie looked up. She'd seen that shape, that hat, those denim-clad legs before.

"Gabe?"

He fired another shot, bringing the musicians to a stop and capturing the attention of all the dancers.

"I'm taking you hostage, ma'am," he said, stalking Jessie and taking her by the arm. "Just come with me, and nobody will be hurt."

"What are you doing, Gabe?"

"I'm an outlaw, kidnapping my woman," he said with a snarl. "And I'm ready to deal with anyone who says different, including her."

Even Jessie wasn't prepared for the kiss he planted on her parted lips.

Even Gabe wasn't prepared for the involuntary response he got.

Moments later she was astride the horse, being gathered into Gabe's arms. "Let's go, Blaze, just like Horace told you," Gabe said, firing one last shot for effect.

The onlookers glanced toward the sheriff's office, expecting to see him intervene. Instead, they watched as the man wearing the badge gave the kidnapper a salute as he rode out of town.

"All right, Gabe," Jessie said. "You can put me down now. The tourists have been entertained."

"I wasn't entertaining the tourists, ma'am. I was doing some serious kidnapping."

"And I'm doing some serious protesting."

"You're entirely too serious, Jessie," Gabe said, in his best John Wayne imitation, "that's always been your problem. You ought to loosen up and let go every now and then. You'd be surprised to find out how much fun it is."

Jessie's mouth flew open.

Blaze left the road and plunged into the woods, heading straight up the mountain.

In stunned disbelief Jessie hung on. This was the Gabe she remembered from childhood, the one she'd lost in the years since. She leaned back against him, glorying in the feel of his arms around her, sliding shamelessly into the V between his legs, trying not to feel his breath against the side of her cheek.

For some thirty minutes they traveled that way, with every upward movement pushing her back against Gabe and every downward movement bringing him tight against her.

"Where are we going?" she finally asked breathlessly.

"I'm taking you to a special place, a place I don't think you've ever been before."

"There isn't much of this mountain I haven't covered, Gabriel St. Clair."

"That's what I would have said once. But I'd have been wrong too."

Jessie gasped. "You wrong? I don't believe that."

The ride had become a mad challenge. Tree limbs reached out, snagging Jessie's dance-hall-girl costume, jerking the feather from her hair as they plunged recklessly through the brush.

"Careful, Blaze," Gabe admonished, "we don't want to injure our victim before we get to the hideout."

Jessie's gasp turned into a hoot of glee. "Hideout? You can't be planning to ransom me—who do you think will care one way or another whether I'm rescued?"

"Jane and Lonnie, Nathan, Mike, and your band, who, incidentally, are being invited by your record producer to go to Nashville with you to make your record."

"But I'm not going to Nashville," she protested, burrowing against Gabe as a vicious vine caught the last of her skirt and ripped it from her legs. "I'm not leaving Pumpkinvine Mountain."

"Not permanently," he agreed, as Blaze left the woods, trotting into a small clearing.

She would have continued the argument if she hadn't caught sight of the cabin. There was smoke coming from the chimney, and the windows were open, allowing a ruffle of white curtain to move gracefully in the breeze.

"Who lives here?" she asked.

"Nobody lives here. According to Uncle Buck, it's been empty for nearly fifty years."

"Uncle Buck?"

He slid to the ground and held out his arms. "Come inside, Jessie, and I'll tell you about Sanctuary."

She slipped into his arms, hung there for a moment, then let go. "Sanctuary?"

"Come inside, Jess. You'll see."

Intrigued, she followed him, pausing to let her eyes play across the valley as she took in the view from the porch. Inside the cabin there was a fire smoldering in the rock fireplace. The odor of something delicious wafted in the air.

Gabe struck a match and touched it to the wick of a lamp with a cloudy pink chimney, throwing a warm glow across the interior.

"I don't understand," Jessie said softly, caught up in the emotions swirling around the room. "I feel as if I ought to whisper, as if this is some special place."

"It is, Jessie, it's the cabin where my grandmother and your grandfather met. This is what was sealed off, protected from the outside world. This is the true sanctuary of your mountain. This is what you've been trying to preserve without knowing it."

"Yes," she murmured, walking around, touching the desk, the book of poetry, the back of the rocker. "How'd you know?"

"I didn't. I stumbled on it accidentally, and once I'd spent the night here, I finally understood."

Jessie turned back to Gabe, afraid to ask what it was that he understood.

"Uncle Buck wanted to sell this land because it brought him pain. You see, he loved Martha too. First she picked his brother, then your grandfather. After his brother died, Buck thought she'd turn to him. She didn't. She died, of guilt and a broken heart."

"Martha must have been a very special woman."

"A lot like you, Buck said. But he was wrong about selling. He thought if he brought in new people, he'd make his pain go away. As long as the cabin was here, that hurt just intensified until it turned him into a lonely old man."

"How sad. Four people caught by fate in lives they couldn't change. Now that he's thinking of selling all the St. Clair land, maybe he'll find some happiness with Effie."

"I can't sell this land, Jessie," he said, answering her unvoiced question. "Martha deliberately sold the land around it, and your grandfather held on to the strip that offered the only entrance."

"You called it Sanctuary."

"I think it is," Gabe answered, taking a step toward her and closing the door behind him. "It was our grandparents' sanctuary, and now it's ours."

"I don't understand," she said. But she did. And it wasn't the house, the warm glow of the lamp, the fire, that were bringing the curious sense of peace and belonging.

It was the love stored inside.

And the love in Gabe's eyes.

And the love in Jessie's heart.

"You see, Jess, when they sealed off the entrance, they kept their love safe for all time. Now it's our place. I love you, Jessie. If you want to stay here, I'll stay. I'm not leaving you again."

All her pain fell away, and Jessie felt as light and free as the air. She wanted to dance. She wanted to sing, not sad, hurting songs, but songs of love found, reclaimed, renewed.

"Are you saying that this is our place, Gabriel St. Clair?"

"It is, if you'll share it."

"And you think a guardian angel can live with the outlaw he's sworn to restrain?"

"I think so, if the outlaw is properly repentant for her sins."

"She is," Jessie agreed vehemently. "I apologize for telling Laura that I was pregnant so she'd drop you that last summer before you left for college, and for letting her father think you were about to run away together."

"You did what?"

"Actually, I wrote him a note. Of course I shouldn't have used notebook paper. I never was sure he took it seriously."

"He did."

"And I'll apologize to Uncle Buck for telling the Bureau of Alcohol and Tobacco about his last still," she went on.

"And what else?" Gabe asked, taking a step closer.

"I can't think of anything else, except maybe"—she took a long breath—"keeping it a secret that after Martha died, Pop found a new vein of gold on your land, right where he thought it might be. It didn't cross over into ours, and he felt as if he'd already done enough for the St. Clairs. He tried to buy the land from your uncle, who refused to sell, so he didn't tell him."

Gabe gave a disbelieving laugh. "You're kidding. Why didn't your dad do something?"

"He never believed Pop. He thought it was another of his pipe dreams. But now, you're rich, Gabriel St. Clair, thanks to the Jameses."

"That's the truth. They gave me you."

"No, I mean money. You have a gold mine that should be the biggest producer since they first discovered gold here."

"You mean *we're* rich, Jessie? That mountain is going to make us rich?"

"This mountain has always made us rich, Gabe."

He looked at her for a long moment. "We can go anywhere we want, do anything we want, and we'll always have this to come home to."

Jessie sagged against Gabriel, lifting her arms to encircle his neck. She could have blamed it on the spell of the cabin, but she'd have been lying. She could have said that this was one kiss for the road, but she didn't think there was one. She could have told him that she'd already packed her bag and made arrangements for Nathan to run the saloon while she was away going after the man she loved, but she hadn't had to leave her mountain. The man she loved had brought her to its summit.

"I tried so hard to get away," Gabe said, "to find something, someone to love me. And all the time it was here. I've been such a fool."

"And I was holding on to what I knew was safe, long after it was gone. I needed love so much that

I tried to buy it. Love, to me, was Pumpkinvine Mountain, where you and I found each other."

"Well, it's yours now, Jess. I give it back to you."

"It wasn't the mountain I wanted," she admitted. "It never really was. Love is anywhere you are, Gabriel St. Clair."

This time she kissed him. This time it was Jessie who unbuttoned and removed Gabe's shirt, planting little smacks across his chest and down his stomach until her mouth collided with his belt. Then that was gone, along with his boots, jeans, and underwear.

The bed seemed to welcome them, curling in around them as they sank into the new feather mattress, obliterating the sound of the outside world and fanning the fires of their passion.

"Are you sure, Gabe?" she asked, taking his bottom lip between her teeth, inching upward until she was astride him. "I won't let you leave me again."

"I'm sure," he murmured between groans and the uncontrollable undulation of his body against hers. He hadn't been certain that he was doing the right thing. Now, looking up at her, face flushed, eyes closed in triumph, he played with her bottom, still covered with silk, with her legs, still covered with mesh stockings. "I'm sure you're wearing too many clothes."

"Take them off," she directed as she shimmied from her panties, unzipped the costume, peeled it from her body with a shiver that freed her breasts, and took away the last of his breath and his reason.

Hot kisses. Hot bodies. Hot sex.

He gasped when she came to her knees and lifted herself over him, taking him inside her so that he filled her completely.

After that, they began to fly, reaching for heights beyond the stars on which she wished, beyond the glory for which he'd once strived. Together they soared, as if on wings of joy, to some bright place where love goes to grow.

"You know," she observed later, as they watched an orange harvest moon rise over the valley, "you said your grandmother sold off the land to seal off the entrance. I think what she was really doing was closing the exit."

"Does it matter now? I mean, since a St. Clair is marrying a James, and that makes everything right."

Jessie sat up, the sheet falling from her nude body. "Whoa! A James is marrying a St. Clair? Did I miss something here?"

"I hope not, outlaw. I love you, and I never want you to miss anything again."

"About that proposal. I think you'd better repeat it. I must have been sleeping or something."

"Or something," he said with a smile in his voice. "Something I plan to make sure you continue to enjoy in vast, giant, large amounts. What do you say, Jessie James?"

She leaned her head back, gazing into laughing blue eyes, and knew that she'd found her best friend, and her only love, again. "I say yes! Yes! Yes! I love you, Gabriel St. Clair, and I'll marry you whenever and wherever you say."

He tugged her back in his arms. "Now, as to the particulars. We'll keep this place as our home base, our sanctuary, the place where we replenish our souls. From here, we'll take that road we're going to build across your property and go wherever we want to go. We can drive up to Nashville to make your record and come back when you're famished."

"Don't you mean finished?"

He kissed her nose. "No, I mean famished, starved for this place, your mountain and me."

She returned his kiss by planting one of her own on his chin. "And we can get the new mine into production, unless," she said anxiously, "you'd rather keep on being a G-man."

"No, I've already handed in my resignation. Ben was sorry to lose me, but he understood. I told him I was thinking of running for mayor."

"Good," she said, sighing as she snuggled closer. "What about children? I've always dreamed of having children."

"As many and as often as you like. As a matter of fact, I wouldn't mind doing a bit more toward making your dreams come true, right now."

As he pushed himself to one elbow, he gazed down at the beautiful woman who'd always been there for him. Outside the window he heard a noise that fell somewhere between the honk of a goose with laryngitis and a lovesick moose.

"Horace," he yelled, "I hear you out there. You and Daisy make yourself at home in the barn with Blaze. We're not ready to leave yet."

"And Daisy?" Jessie repeated with a grin.

"Of course. Who do you think gave me the idea? Horace kidnapped his woman, I kidnapped mine. Now about the honeymoon, what would you think of New Guinea?"

"New Guinea? Why on earth would you want to go there?"

"I want to see one of Jane's New Guinea flapdoodle hens in person. She told me they mate for life. I like that idea."

"So do I," Jessie said softly. And, just for a moment, she thought she heard a sigh of pleasure.

Maybe it was residual happiness trapped inside the walls. Then again, maybe it was happiness bubbling over from the woman inside of Jessie who'd finally broken free. Jessie glanced through the window searching for a star and said a silent *thank you*. After all, not many people had their wishes come true—ever.

She didn't mind that hers was fourteen years late.

EPILOGUE

The Lumpkin County Legend
—November 4, 1994

    The wedding of Jessie James and Gabriel St. Clair will long be the talk of Lumpkin County. The unusual ceremony was held in the little Methodist church at the base of Pumpkinvine Mountain. There were some in attendance who regretted the end of the feud between the St. Clairs and the Jameses. Anything that has gone on two hundred years is a tradition not lightly given up by mountain folks.

    Buck St. Clair escorted the bride. Their trek to the altar was made to an interesting arrangement of the wedding march performed by Buck's fiancée Effie Stevens, accompanied by the Dusters, the members of the bride's country-music band.

Members of the wedding party included the matron of honor, Jane Couples Short, the best man, cousin of the groom Joey St. Clair, and usher Lonnie Short. The reception, held in the Gold Dust Saloon, property of the bride, provided a surprise visit from hometown boy Governor Diller and his lovely wife, Regina.

But it was agreed by all that the most memorable part of the event, other than the kiss between the bride and the groom, was their unusual method of departure from the reception. Instead of the customary vehicle adorned with tin cans and good wishes written on the windshield in shoe polish, Mr. and Mrs. St. Clair ran through a cordon of rice throwers and climbed on the back of a large brown mule named Horace, who was said to have been, to a large extent, responsible for the wedding.

Accompanying the flower-bedecked mule was a small white horse wearing a yellow straw hat with golden daises around the brim. The departure was truly unique, as was the bride's wedding gift to the groom—a crate tied up with ribbons and strapped to the horse's back, containing what appeared to this writer to be a very strange-looking chicken. The groom confided with great pride that the bird was a rare and precious species, a New Guinea flapdoodle hen.

THE EDITOR'S CORNER

The coming month brings to mind lions and lambs—
not only because of the weather but also because of our
six wonderful LOVESWEPTs. In these books you'll find
fierce and feisty, warm and gentle characters who add
up to a rich and exciting array of people whose stories
of falling in love are enthralling.

Judy Gill starts things off this month with another
terrific story in **KISS AND MAKE UP,** LOVESWEPT
#678. He'd never been around when they were mar-
ried, but now that Kat Waddell has decided to hire
a nanny to help with the kids, her ex-husband, Rand,
insists he's perfect for the job! Accepting his offer means
letting him live in the basement apartment—too dangerously close for a man whose presence arouses potent
memories of reckless passion . . . and painful images of
love gone wrong. He married Kat hoping for the perfect fantasy family, but the pretty picture he'd imagined
didn't include an unhappy wife he never seemed to sat-

isfy . . . except in bed. Now Rand needs to show Kat he's changed. The sensual magic he weaves makes her feel cherished at last, but Kat wonders if it's enough to mend their broken vows. Judy's special touch makes this story of love reborn especially poignant.

It's on to Scotland for **LORD OF THE ISLAND**, LOVESWEPT #679, by the wonderfully talented Kimberli Wagner. Ian MacLeod is annoyed by the American woman who comes to stay on Skye during the difficult winter months, but when Tess Hartley sheds her raingear, the laird is enchanted by the dark-eyed siren whose fiery temper reveals a rebel who won't be ordered around by any man—even him! He expects pity, even revulsion at the evidence of his terrible accident, but Tess's pain runs as deep as his does, and her artist's eye responds to Ian's scarred face with wonder at his courage . . . and a wildfire hunger to lose herself in his arms. As always, Kimberli weaves an intense story of love and triumph you won't soon forget.

Victoria Leigh gives us a hero who is rough, rugged, and capable of **DANGEROUS LOVE**, LOVESWEPT #680. Four years earlier, he'd fallen in love with her picture, but when Luke Sinclair arrives on her secluded island to protect his boss's sister from the man who'd once kidnapped her, he is stunned to find that Elisabeth Connor is more exquisite than he'd dreamed—and not nearly as fragile as he'd feared. Instead, she warms to the fierce heat of his gaze, begging to know the ecstacy of his touch. Even though he's sworn to protect her with his life, Elisabeth must make him see that she wants him to share it with her instead. Only Victoria could deliver a romance that's as sexy and fun as it is touching.

We're delighted to have another fabulous book from Laura Taylor this month, and **WINTER HEART**, LOVESWEPT #681, is Laura at her best. Suspicious that the elegant blonde has a hidden agenda when she hires him to restore a family mansion, Jack McMillan quickly puts Mariah Chandler on the defensive—and is shocked to feel a flash flood of heat and desire rush through him! He believes she is only a spoiled rich girl indulging a whim, but he can't deny the hunger that ignites within him to possess her. Tantalized by sensual longings she's never expected to feel, Mariah surrenders to the dizzying pleasure of Jack's embrace. She's fought her demons by helping other women who have suffered but has never told Jack of the shadows that still haunt her nights. Now Mariah must heal his wounded spirit by finally sharing her pain and daring him to share a future.

Debra Dixon brings together a hot, take-charge Cajun and a sizzling TV seductress in **MIDNIGHT HOUR,** LOVESWEPT #682. Her voice grabs his soul and turns him inside out before he even sees her, but when Dr. Nick Devereaux gazes at Midnight Mercy Malone, the town's TV horror-movie hostess, he aches to muss her gorgeous russet hair . . . and make love to the lady until she moans his name! Still, he likes her even better out of her slinky costumes, an everyday enchantress who tempts him to make regular house calls. His sexy accent gives her goosebumps, but Mercy hopes her lusty alter ego might scare off a man she fears will choose work over her. Yet, his kisses send her up in flames and make her ache for love that never ends. Debra's spectacular romance will leave you breathless.

Olivia Rupprecht invites you to a **SHOTGUN WEDDING,** LOVESWEPT #683. Aaron Breedlove once fled his mountain hamlet to escape his desire for Addy McDonald, but now fate has brought him back— and his father's deathbed plea has given him no choice but to keep the peace between the clans and marry his dangerous obsession! With hair as dark as a moonlit night, Addy smells of wildflowers and rainwater, and Aaron can deny his anguished passion no longer. He is the knight in shining armor she's always dreamed of, but Addy yearns to become his wife in every way—and

Aaron refuses to accept her gift or surrender his soul. **SHOTGUN WEDDING** is a sensual, steamy romance that Olivia does like no one else.

Happy reading,

With warmest wishes,

Nita Taublib

Nita Taublib

Associate Publisher

P.S. Don't miss the spectacular women's novels coming from Bantam in April: **DARK PARADISE** is the dangerously erotic novel of romantic suspense from nationally bestselling author Tami Hoag; **WARRIOR BRIDE** is a sizzling medieval romance in the bestselling tradition of Julie Garwood from Tamara Leigh, a dazzling new author; **REBEL IN SILK** is the fabulous new *Once Upon a Time* romance from bestselling Loveswept author Sandra Chastain. We'll be giving you a sneak peek at these terrific books in next month's LOVESWEPTs. And immediately following this page, look for a preview of the spectacular women's fiction books from Bantam *available now*!

Don't miss these exciting books by your
favorite Bantam authors

On sale in February:
*SILK AND
STONE*
by Deborah Smith

*LADY
DANGEROUS*
by Suzanne Robinson

*SINS OF
INNOCENCE*
by Jean Stone

"A uniquely significant voice in contemporary women's fiction."
—*Romantic Times*

Deborah Smith

SILK AND STONE

From Miracle *to* Blue Willow, *Deborah Smith's evocative novels have won a special place in readers' hearts. Now comes a spellbinding, unforgettably romantic new work. Vibrant with wit, aching with universal emotion,* SILK AND STONE *is Deborah Smith at her most triumphant . . .*

She had everything ready for him, everything but herself. What could she say to a husband she hadn't seen or spoken to in ten years: *Hi, honey, how'd your decade go?*

The humor was nervous, and morbid. She knew that. Samantha Raincrow hurt for him, hurt in ways she couldn't put into words. Ten years of waiting, of thinking about what he was going through, of *why* he'd been subjected to it, had worn her down to bare steel.

What he'd endured would always be her fault.

She moved restlessly around the finest hotel suite in the city, obsessed with straightening fresh flowers that were already perfectly arranged in their vases. He wouldn't have seen many flowers. She wanted him to remember the scent of youth and freedom. Of love.

Broad windows looked out over Raleigh. A nice city for a reunion. The North Carolina summer had just begun; the trees still wore the dark shades of new spring leaves.

She wanted everything to be new for him, but knew it could never be, that they were both haunted by the past—betrayals that couldn't be undone. She was Alexandra Lomax's niece; she couldn't scrub that stain out of her blood.

Her gifts were arranged around the suite's sitting room; Sam went to them and ran her hands over each one. A silk tapestry, six-feet-square and woven in geometrics from an old Cherokee design, was draped over a chair. She wanted him to see one of the ways she'd spent all the hours alone. Lined up in a precise row along one wall were five large boxes filled with letters she'd written to him and never sent, because he wouldn't have read them. A journal of every day. On a desk in front of the windows were stacks of bulging photo albums. One was filled with snapshots of her small apartment in California, the car she'd bought second-hand, years ago, and still drove, more of her tapestries, and her loom. And the Cove. Pictures of the wild Cove, and the big log house where he'd been born. She wanted him to see how lovingly she'd cared for it over the years.

The other albums were filled with her modeling portfolio. A strange one, by most standards. Just hands. Her hands, the only beautiful thing about her, holding soaps and perfumes and jewelry, caressing lingerie and detergent and denture cleaner, and a thousand other products. Because she wanted him to understand everything about her work, she'd brought the DeMeda book, too—page after over-sized, sensual page of black-and-white art photos. Photos of her fingertips touching a man's glistening, naked back, or molded to the crest of a muscular, bare thigh.

If he cared, she would explain about the ludi-crous amount of money she'd gotten for that work, and that the book had been created by a famous photographer, and was considered an art form. If he cared, she'd assure him that there was nothing pro-vocative about standing under hot studio lights with her hands cramping, while beautiful, half-clothed male models yawned and told her about their latest boyfriends.

If he cared.

Last, she went to a small, rectangular folder on a coffee table near the room's sofa. She sat down and opened it, her hands shaking so badly she could barely grasp the folder. The new deed for the Cove, with both his name and hers on it, was neatly tucked inside. She'd promised to transfer title to him the day he came home. If she hadn't held her ownership of the Cove over him like a threat all these years, he would have divorced her.

She hadn't promised to let him have it without her.

Sam hated that coercion, and knew he hated it, too. It was too much like something her Aunt Alexandra would have done. But Sam would not lose him, not without fighting for a second chance.

The phone rang. She jumped up, scattering the paperwork on the carpet, and ran to answer. "Dreyfus delivery service," said a smooth, elegantly drawling voice. "I have one slightly-used husband for you, ma'am."

Their lawyer's black sense of humor didn't help matters. Her heart pounded, and she felt dizzy. "Ben, you're downstairs?"

"Yes, in the lobby. Actually, I'm in the lobby. He's in the men's room, changing clothes."

"*Changing clothes?*"

"He asked me to stop on the way here. I perform many functions, Sam, but helping my clients pick a new outfit is a first."

"Why in the world—"

"He didn't want you to see him in what they gave him to wear. In a manner of speaking, he wanted to look like a civilian, again."

Sam inhaled raggedly and bowed her head, pressing her fingertips under her eyes, pushing hard. She wouldn't cry, wouldn't let him see her for the first time in ten years with her face swollen and her nose running. Small dignities were all she had left. "Has he said anything?" she asked, when she could trust herself to speak calmly.

"Hmmm, lawyer-client confidentiality, Sam. I represent both of you. What kind of lawyer do you think I am? Never mind, I don't want to hear the brutal truth."

"One who's become a good friend."

Ben hesitated. "Idle flattery." Then, slowly, "He said he would walk away without ever seeing you, again, if he could."

She gripped the phone numbly. *That's no worse than you expected*, she told herself. But she felt dead inside. "Tell him the doors to the suite will be open."

"All right. I'm sure he needs all the open doors he can get."

"I can't leave them all open. If I did, I'd lose him." Ben didn't ask what she meant; he'd helped her engineer some of those closed doors.

"Parole is not freedom," Ben said. "He understands that."

"And I'm sure he's thrilled that he's being forced to live with a wife he doesn't want."

"I suspect he doesn't know what he wants, at the moment."

"He's always known, Ben. That's the problem."

She said good-bye, put the phone down and walked with leaden resolve to the suite's double doors. She opened them and stepped back. For a moment, she considered checking herself in a mirror one last time, turned halfway, then realized she was operating on the assumption that what she looked like mattered to him. So she faced the doors and waited.

Each faint whir and rumble of the elevators down the hall made her nerves dance. She could barely breathe, listening for the sound of those doors opening. She smoothed her upswept hair, then anxiously fingered a blond strand that had escaped. Jerking at each hair, she pulled them out. A dozen or more, each unwilling to go. If it hurt, she didn't notice.

She clasped her hands in front of her pale yellow suitdress, then unclasped them, fiddled with the gold braid along the neck, twisted the plain gold wedding band on her left hand. She never completely removed it from her body, even when she worked. It had either remained on her finger or on a sturdy gold chain around her neck, all these years.

That chain, lying coldly between her breasts, also held his wedding ring.

She heard the hydraulic purr of an elevator settling into place, then the softer rush of metal doors sliding apart. Ten years compressed in the nerve-wracking space of a few seconds. If he weren't the one walking up the long hall right now, if some unsuspecting stranger strolled by instead, she thought her shaking legs would collapse.

Damn the thick carpeting. She couldn't gauge his steps. She wasn't ready. No, she would always be ready. Her life stopped, and she was waiting, waiting . . .

He walked into the doorway and halted. This tall, broad-shouldered stranger was her husband. Every memory she had of his appearance was there, stamped with a brutal decade of maturity, but there. Except for the look in his eyes. Nothing had ever been bleak and hard about him before. He stared at her with an intensity that could have burned her shadow on the floor.

Words were hopeless, but all that they had. "Welcome back," she said. Then, brokenly, "*Jake.*"

He took a deep breath, as if a shiver had run through him. He closed the doors without ever taking his eyes off her. Then he was at her in two long steps, grasping her by the shoulders, lifting her to her toes. They were close enough to share a breath, a heartbeat. "I trained myself not to think about you," he said, his voice a raw whisper. "Because if I had, I would have lost my mind."

"I never deserted you. I wanted to be part of your life, but you wouldn't let me. Will you please try now?"

"Do you still have it?" he asked.

Anger. Defeat. The hoarse sound she made contained both. "Yes."

He released her. "Good. That's all that matters."

Sam turned away, tears coming helplessly. After all these years, there was still only one thing he wanted from her, and it was the one thing she hated, a symbol of pride and obsession she would never understand, a blood-red stone that had controlled the lives of too many people already, including theirs.

The Pandora ruby.

LADY DANGEROUS
by
Suzanne Robinson

"An author with star quality . . . spectacularly talented."
—*Romantic Times*

Liza Elliot had a very good reason for posing as a maid in the house of the notorious Viscount Radcliffe. It was the only way the daring beauty could discover whether this sinister nobleman had been responsible for her brother's murder. But Liza never knew how much she risked until the night she came face-to-face with the dangerously arresting and savagely handsome viscount himself . . .

Iron squealed against iron as the footmen swung the gates back again. Black horses trotted into view, two pairs, drawing a black lacquered carriage. Liza stirred uneasily as she realized that vehicle, tack, and coachman were all in unrelieved black. Polished brass lanterns and fittings provided the only contrast.

The carriage pulled up before the house, the horses stamping and snorting in the cold. The coachman, wrapped in a driving coat and muffled in a black scarf, made no sound as he controlled the ill-tempered menace of his animals. She couldn't help leaning forward a bit, in spite of her growing trepidation. Perhaps it was the eeriness of the fog-drenched night, or the unnerving appearance of the shining black and silent carriage, but no one moved.

Then she saw it. A boot. A black boot unlike any she'd ever seen. High of heel, tapered in the toe, scuffed, and sticking out of the carriage window. Its owner must be reclining inside. As she closed her mouth, which had fallen open, Liza saw a puff of smoke billow out from the interior. So aghast was she at this unorthodox arrival, she didn't hear the duke and his brother come down the steps to stand near her.

Suddenly the boot was withdrawn. The head footman immediately jumped forward and opened the carriage door. The interior lamps hadn't been lit. From the darkness stepped a man so tall, he had to curl almost double to keep his hat from hitting the roof of the vehicle.

The footman retreated as the man straightened. Liza sucked in her breath, and a feeling of unreality swamped her other emotions. The man who stood before her wore clothing so dark, he seemed a part of the night and the gloom of the carriage that had borne him. A low-crowned hat with a wide brim concealed his face, and he wore a long coat that flared away from his body. It was open, and he brushed one edge of it back where it revealed buckskin pants, a vest, a black, low-slung belt and holster bearing a gleaming revolver.

He paused, undisturbed by the shock he'd created. Liza suddenly remembered a pamphlet she'd seen on the American West. That's where she'd seen a man like this. Not anywhere in England, but in illustrations of the American badlands.

At last the man moved. He struck a match on his belt and lit a thin cigar. The tip glowed, and for a moment his face was revealed in the light of the match. She glimpsed black, black hair, so dark it seemed to absorb the flame of the match. Thick lashes lifted to reveal the glitter of cat-green eyes, a straight nose, and a chin that bore a day's stubble. The match died and was tossed aside. The man hooked his thumbs in his belt and sauntered down the line of servants, ignoring them.

He stopped in front of the duke, puffed on the cigar, and stared at the older man. Slowly, a pretense of a smile spread over his face. He removed the cigar from his mouth, shoved his hat back on his head, and spoke for the first time.

"Well, well, well. Evening, Daddy."

That accent, it was so strange—a hot, heavy drawl spiked with cool and nasty amusement. This man took his time with words, caressed them, savored them, and made his enemies wait in apprehension for him to complete them. The duke bristled, and his white hair almost stood out like a lion's mane as he gazed at his son.

"Jocelin, you forget yourself."

The cigar sailed to the ground and hissed as it hit the damp pavement. Liza longed to shrink back from the sudden viciousness that sprang from the viscount's eyes. The viscount smiled again and spoke softly, with relish and an evil amusement. The drawl vanished, to be supplanted by a clipped, aristocratic accent.

"I don't forget. I'll never forget. Forgetting is your vocation, one you've elevated to a sin, or you wouldn't bring my dear uncle where I could get my hands on him."

All gazes fastened on the man standing behind the duke. Though much younger than his brother, Yale Marshall had the same thick hair, black as his brother's had once been, only gray at the temples. Of high stature like his nephew, he reminded Liza of the illustrations of knights in *La Morte d'Arthur*, for he personified doomed beauty and chivalry. He had the same startling green eyes as his nephew, and he gazed at the viscount sadly as the younger man faced him.

Yale murmured to his brother, "I told you I shouldn't have come."

With knightly dignity he stepped aside, and the movement brought him nearer to his nephew. Jocelin's left hand touched the revolver on his hip as his uncle turned. The duke hissed his name, and the hand dropped loosely to his side. He lit another cigar.

At a glance from his face, the butler suddenly sprang into motion. He ran up the steps to open the door. The duke marched after him, leaving his son to follow, slowly, after taking a few leisurely puffs on his cigar.

"Ah, well," he murmured. "I can always kill him later."

SINS OF INNOCENCE
by
JEAN STONE

They were four women with only one thing in common: each gave up her baby to a stranger. They'd met in a home for unwed mothers, where all they had to hold on to was each other. Now, twenty-five years later, it's time to go back and face the past. The date is set for a reunion with the children they have never known. But who will find the courage to attend?

"I've decided to find my baby," Jess said.

Susan picked up a spoon and stirred in a hefty teaspoon of sugar from the bowl. She didn't usually take sugar, but she needed to keep her hands busy. Besides, if she tried to drink from the mug now, she'd probably drop it.

"What's that got to do with me?"

Jess took a sip, then quickly put down the mug. It's probably still too hot, Susan thought. She probably burned the Estée Lauder right off her lips.

"I . . ." The woman stammered, not looking Susan in the eye, "I was wondering if you've ever had the same feelings."

The knot that had found its way into Susan's stomach increased in size.

"I have a son," Susan said.

Jess looked into her mug. "So do I. In fact, I have two sons and a daughter. And"—she picked up the mug to try again—"a husband."

Susan pushed back her hair. *My* baby, she thought. *David's baby.* She closed her eyes, trying to envision what he would look like today. He'd be a man. Older even than David had been when . . .

How could she tell Jess that 1968 had been the biggest regret of her life? How could she tell this woman she no longer knew that she felt the decisions she'd made then had led her in a direction that had no definition, no purpose? But years ago Susan had accepted one important thing: She couldn't go back.

"So why do you want to do this?"

Jess looked across the table at Susan. "Because it's time," she said.

Susan hesitated before asking the next question. "What do you want from me?"

Jess set down her mug and began twisting the ring again. "Haven't you ever wondered? About your baby?"

Only a million times. Only every night when I go to bed. Only every day as I've watched Mark grow and blossom. Only every time I see a boy who is the same age.

"What are you suggesting?"

"I'm planning a reunion. With our children. I've seen Miss Taylor, and she's agreed to help. She knows where they all are."

"*All* of them?"

"Yours. Mine. P.J.'s and Ginny's. I'm going to

contact everyone, even the kids. Whoever shows up, shows up. Whoever doesn't, doesn't. It's a chance we'll all be taking, but we'll be doing it together. *Together*. The way we got through it in the first place."

The words hit Susan like a rapid fire of a BB gun at a carnival. She stood and walked across the room. She straightened the stack of laundry. "I think you're out of your mind," she said.

And don't miss these heart-stopping
romances from Bantam Books,
on sale in March:

DARK PARADISE
by the nationally bestselling author
Tami Hoag
"Tami Hoag belongs at the top of
everyone's favorite author list"
—*Romantic Times*

WARRIOR BRIDE
by **Tamara Leigh**
" . . . a passionate love story that captures all
the splendor of the medieval era."
—nationally bestselling author
Teresa Medeiros

REBEL IN SILK
by **Sandra Chastain**
"Sandra Chastain's characters' steamy
relationships are the stuff dreams are
made of."
—*Romantic Times*

OFFICIAL RULES

To enter the sweepstakes below carefully follow all instructions found elsewhere in this offer.

The **Winners Classic** will award prizes with the following approximate maximum values: 1 Grand Prize: $26,500 (or $25,000 cash alternate); 1 First Prize: $3,000; 5 Second Prizes: $400 each; 35 Third Prizes: $100 each; 1,000 Fourth Prizes: $7.50 each. Total maximum retail value of Winners Classic Sweepstakes is $42,500. Some presentations of this sweepstakes may contain individual entry numbers corresponding to one or more of the aforementioned prize levels. To determine the Winners, individual entry numbers will first be compared with the winning numbers preselected by computer. For winning numbers not returned, prizes will be awarded in random drawings from among all eligible entries received. Prize choices may be offered at various levels. If a winner chooses an automobile prize, all license and registration fees, taxes, destination charges and, other expenses not offered herein are the responsibility of the winner. If a winner chooses a trip, travel must be complete within one year from the time the prize is awarded. Minors must be accompanied by an adult. Travel companion(s) must also sign release of liability. Trips are subject to space and departure availability. Certain black-out dates may apply.

The following applies to the sweepstakes named above:

No purchase necessary. You can also enter the sweepstakes by sending your name and address to: P.O. Box 508, Gibbstown, N.J. 08027. Mail each entry separately. Sweepstakes begins 6/1/93. Entries must be received by 12/30/94. Not responsible for lost, late, damaged, misdirected, illegible or postage due mail. Mechanically reproduced entries are not eligible. All entries become property of the sponsor and will not be returned.

Prize Selection/Validations: Selection of winners will be conducted no later than 5:00 PM on January 28, 1995, by an independent judging organization whose decisions are final. Random drawings will be held at 1211 Avenue of the Americas, New York, N.Y. 10036. Entrants need not be present to win. Odds of winning are determined by total number of entries received. Circulation of this sweepstakes is estimated not to exceed 200 million. All prizes are guaranteed to be awarded and delivered to winners. Winners will be notified by mail and may be required to complete an affidavit of eligibility and release of liability which must be returned within 14 days of date on notification or alternate winners will be selected in a random drawing. Any prize notification letter or any prize returned to a participating sponsor, Bantam Doubleday Dell Publishing Group, Inc., its participating divisions or subsidiaries, or the independent judging organization as undeliverable will be awarded to an alternate winner. Prizes are not transferable. No substitution for prizes except as offered or as may be necessary due to unavailability, in which case a prize of equal or greater value will be awarded. Prizes will be awarded approximately 90 days after the drawing. All taxes are the sole responsibility of the winners. Entry constitutes permission (except where prohibited by law) to use winners' names, hometowns, and likenesses for publicity purposes without further or other compensation. Prizes won by minors will be awarded in the name of parent or legal guardian.

Participation: Sweepstakes open to residents of the United States and Canada, except for the province of Quebec. Sweepstakes sponsored by Bantam Doubleday Dell Publishing Group, Inc., (BDD), 1540 Broadway, New York, NY 10036. Versions of this sweepstakes with different graphics and prize choices will be offered in conjunction with various solicitations or promotions by different subsidiaries and divisions of BDD. Where applicable, winners will have their choice of any prize offered at level won. Employees of BDD, its divisions, subsidiaries, advertising agencies, independent judging organization, and their immediate family members are not eligible.

Canadian residents, in order to win, must first correctly answer a time limited arithmetical skill testing question. Void in Puerto Rico, Quebec and wherever prohibited or restricted by law. Subject to all federal, state, local and provincial laws and regulations. For a list of major prize winners (available after 1/29/95): send a self-addressed, stamped envelope entirely separate from your entry to: Sweepstakes Winners, P.O. Box 517, Gibbstown, NJ 08027. Requests must be received by 12/30/94. DO NOT SEND ANY OTHER CORRESPONDENCE TO THIS P.O. BOX.